Her Cowboy Boss

Arlene James

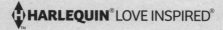

HARLEQUIN® LOVE INSPIRED®

LOVE INSPIRED BOOKS

Recycling programs for this product may not exist in your area.

ISBN-13: 978-0-373-89940-1

Her Cowboy Boss

After Job had prayed for his friends, the Lord
restored his fortunes and gave him
twice as much as he had before.
—*Job* 42:10

Chapter One

"Stop fussing, Meredith," Wes Billings rasped. "You look as tired as I feel and need to rest now."

Meri sighed and smoothed the covers over her father's chest once more. The weeklong trip to Oklahoma City for his final scheduled chemotherapy treatment had been grueling, and, no doubt, he was as glad as she was to be back at Straight Arrow Ranch.

She prayed that the drugs, which had followed extensive surgery, had done their work and rid her father's rangy six-foot-four-inch body of any remaining cancer. Only time and tests would tell, as Meri, a nurse, well knew. Still, time seemed to slip through her fingers with alarming speed. Her leave of absence from her job at the hospital in the city would soon end, and she would be forced to return there to work.

The irony struck deep as she bent and kissed her dad's bald head through the paper mask that she wore. Meredith had never wanted to leave home. She'd settled on nursing after her mother's unexpected death more than four years earlier, only to discover that her chosen career left her few employment options within driving distance of the tiny town of War Bonnet, some six miles from the ranch. Neither her older brother nor her sister had intended to return permanently to their hometown, yet they'd both recently married locally and settled in to live there, while Meri had come up empty—again—in her search for a job that would allow her to remain near her family.

She disliked living in a large city for many reasons. The summers were hotter and the winters dirtier. Everything was more expensive. Green spaces were few and far too formal. She'd never thought to miss a red-dirt road so much. As time had passed, the hundred miles between War Bonnet and Oklahoma City had started to seem like thousands to her. Moreover, the quality and quantity of medical care to be found there had robbed the smaller communities of hospitals and clinics even this far out, which meant that she couldn't find a job closer to home.

How she hated to think of going back! The traffic and the noise grated on her, and the crime... She shuddered, touching the scar just above her left breast through her blouse.

If help had arrived even a minute later, she doubted she'd be here. In the city, when not working, she felt virtually trapped in her apartment with her cats.

Make that *cat*. She still grieved the loss of Tux, her black-and-white tom.

"Call out if you need me," she said to her dad, stripping off the mask and gloves. She wore the protective gear to care for her father since his infusions had temporarily demolished his immune system. She dropped them into the receptacle beside the door and left the room, stepping into the back hallway of the sprawling old ranch house where she, her siblings and their father before them had grown to adulthood.

Her five-year-old nephew, Donovan, jumped down from his seat at the kitchen table and raced across the room, throwing himself at her, his fiery red head a blur. "Is Grandpa okay? Did you go shopping? Christmas is coming, ya know, and it's my birthday." It was only

October, but Donovan was already counting the days to his next birthday.

"I might've done some shopping," she answered cagily, sliding a narrowed gaze at the table, where she expected to find his parents. Her eyes snagged instead on the dark head of Stark Burns. Before she could catch them, the words that had popped into her mind slid right out of her mouth. "What's *he* doing here?"

She didn't like Stark Burns. She didn't trust him. In her opinion, he'd let her cat Tux die after it had been injured the day of Rex's wedding. Yes, the cat had been seriously wounded, but she believed that careful surgery and nursing care could have saved it. She'd heard that some veterinarians were too quick to put down animals with serious injuries and that large-animal vets were especially hasty in giving up on small animals. Both of those criticisms seemed to apply to Dr. Burns. Still, her brother, Rex, counted him a friend, and Wes paid him well to look after the livestock on the ranch.

And she'd just been rude. Again. Meri was never rude, except when it came to Dr. Stark Burns. She pulled in a deep breath.

"I—I mean, is there a problem with one of the animals?"

Rex frowned at her as Burns hitched

around in his seat, hanging one long arm over the chair back and turning his head to cut his dark eyes at her. No one could say he wasn't a good-looking man, with that thick, coal-black hair and brooding, hawkish features. Plus, he had to be at least as tall as her dad and looked every bit as comfortable in jeans and boots. He was more slender than either her brother or brother-in-law, and he looked just as fine in a hat, which he had the good manners not to wear at the table. She'd always thought sideburns a ridiculous affectation in a man—and given his last name she'd have advised him against them—but somehow they worked on him, which just made her dislike him all the more.

"Yes," Rex said in reply to her question, shooting a look at their father's closed bedroom door.

Obviously, Rex didn't want to worry Dad. Meri couldn't argue with that. She turned Donovan around and walked the boy to the table. The veterinarian's silent gaze tracked her the whole way. Warily she pulled out a chair and sat, while her sister, Ann, sent Donovan into the living room to play with his little cousin, Bodie. Meredith didn't know if that was because the other adults didn't want Donovan to overhear their conversation or because Stark Burns didn't like children. She'd noticed before that he went out of his way to avoid them.

That way of thinking was foreign to the Billings family. Bodie's natural father had died in a flood before she was even born, and Donovan's mother had abandoned him at birth, but the children were part of the Billings family now. Rex had considered himself Bo's father from the moment he'd married her mom, Callie, and Ann had delighted in playing Donovan's mom even before she'd married his dad, Dean, and become his mother in fact.

"What's going on?" Meredith asked, glancing at the solemn faces around the table.

"It's Soldier," Rex said, referring to their father's beloved stud horse.

They'd loaned the handsome sorrel stud to a friend, another rancher down in Texas, who had mares to breed. The horse had been scheduled to return to the ranch before Wes did. Had he not shown up, failed to perform or returned injured?

Callie, who had come to the ranch as the housekeeper, set a fork and a plate overflowing with apple pie in front of Meri. Smiling her thanks, Meredith picked up her fork. Stark Burns followed suit, his pie already half finished. Meri took a bite, humming in appreciation as she glanced at her sister, Ann. Dean, Ann's husband of two months, snugged an arm around Ann's waist, his chin nuzzling her long red hair. The expressions on their faces were serious enough to have Meri putting down her fork again.

"How bad is it?"

"Soldier didn't look too steady when we got him back from Texas," Ann explained. "Then we found him down this morning."

"Oh, no." A horse that couldn't rise to its feet on its own strength could quickly die, because its organs wouldn't function properly, especially its lungs. A horrible fear struck her. If that horse was dead... She abruptly sat forward again and faced Stark Burns. "What did you do?"

He set down his fork, swallowed and calmly wiped his mouth with a paper napkin before bracing his forearms on the tabletop. "I slung him," he said.

Meri blinked. "Slung him?"

Sitting back, Stark crossed his long legs. "I brought in a hoist and a specially designed sling, got him to his feet, drew some blood for testing and set him up on IV fluids." He crumpled the napkin in his hand and tossed it onto his plate. "It's encephalitis, a particularly virulent strain I've been reading they have down in Texas."

Meri's heart thunked. Encephalitis was a deadly disease. She cast a desperate glance around the table. "Don't we vaccinate for that?"

"Yes," Rex said, "but it wouldn't have covered this strain. This was recently brought up from Venezuela."

Meri put her head in her hands. "This is the last thing Dad needs right now."

"We know it, sis," Ann agreed softly.

"And we're all praying," Dean said.

Burns pushed back his chair and rose. "Horse'll need tending through the night for a while."

Rex nodded. "We'll take turns."

Stark Burns shook his dark head. "Nope. The possibility of pneumonia is too great when a horse has been down. I'll be staying nights."

"Let us know if you need anything," Callie said as Burns's long legs carried him toward the hallway flanking the back staircase.

"I'm used to this," he assured her. "I'll just run back to my place for some gear. See y'all in the morning."

Meri narrowed her eyes as he disappeared from view. She would be keeping a very close watch on him. Maybe he hadn't put down Soldier. Yet. But neither would he—if she could help it—let her father's horse die. The others trusted Dr. Burns implicitly, but they had no medical training. She knew enough to assess the quality of his treatment, and she would do so whether he liked it or not.

Shoving a package of clean paper coveralls into his kit, Stark glanced around the Spartan interior of the small room where he slept most nights, trying to think if he'd forgotten anything. Exhaustion tugged at him, but when did it not? Pushing it aside, he ticked off supplies in his head, listing medications and equipment bundles, his hands gliding over each as he recalled them. The air mattress and sleeping bag were kept in the truck. Deciding that he could use a clean pair of socks, he reached into a drawer. His hand struck the small framed photo that he could not bear to display or resist looking at once he'd touched it.

The smiles always shocked him, especially his own, but there he was, tossing his daughter over his shoulder like a sack of grain, while she squealed and her mother laughed. Belinda's ninth birthday. Such a happy day. He could almost hear her giggles.

Don't drop me, Daddy! Don't drop me!

Hold still then, Belindaworm. Mommy, give her that birthday spanking, and be sure she gets one to grow on.

Except there had been no spanking, and she hadn't grown. It had been a joke, and less than five months later, they'd both been dead.

Words he couldn't forget rang through his mind.

I just want to watch this football game. Then we'll go.

Whatever you think best, sweetheart. We'll leave whenever you're ready.

Ten minutes earlier. If they'd just left ten minutes earlier. The grief, nearly four years old now, swamped him, guilt digging its claws deep.

He swiped his thumb over his daughter's face. He'd studied genetics in college. Dark eyes and hair were supposed to be dominant, but Bel had inherited his dark hair and her mother's sky-blue eyes. His blonde, blue-eyed wife had been all things lovely, but his daughter's combination of light and dark had fascinated him.

He shoved the picture back into the drawer and closed it, snagging his kit from the narrow bed as he whirled away and left the room.

Exhaustion pulled at him, so he took three

cans of energy drink from the refrigerator in the dispensary. He wouldn't get much sleep tonight, but he rarely slept well even when he worked himself to the point of exhaustion. On the other hand, only work and slumber let him escape the emptiness, grief and guilt.

He drove from his place on the edge of War Bonnet back to Straight Arrow Ranch. The Billings place was by far the biggest concern in the area. Two square miles in size and well run, the ranch apparently turned a good profit. Though the comfortable, sprawling old house couldn't hold a candle to the home near Ponca City that Stark had walked away from after the deaths of his family, he couldn't have gone back. He and his wife, Catherine, had built that place, pouring their hearts into every brick, board and stone. He never wanted to see it again.

Parking the truck to the side of the reddirt road that separated the Straight Arrow home from the outbuildings, Stark shouldered his kit and automatically reached for his hat. Thinking better of that, he left the wide-brimmed black felt on the seat and got out.

Cool autumn air washed over him as he reached into the back for his bedroll. He hoisted it onto his shoulder, curling his arm around it, and trudged toward the stables, choosing the lit path on the backside of the building. Coming to the welded metal corral fence, he shoved his backpack and bedroll through the lower rungs and onto the ground, then climbed over and dropped down. He shouldered his gear again before going inside the darkened building. The light at the end of the long row outlined the shapely feminine form standing at Soldier's drooping head.

Meredith Billings was the very last person Stark wanted to see tonight. In fact, she was the last person he wanted to see most days. Those accusatory blue eyes and her obvious disdain pierced him clear through every time. Sighing, he started forward, listening to half-a-dozen horses blow and shift as he walked down the long aisle. She waited, petting the butternut sorrel's neck and casting glances into the dark as Stark drew closer.

He didn't say a word, mostly because he knew it needled her, but partly because this was the first time she'd approached him in private. She obviously had something on her mind. He waited for her to come to the point as he carefully stowed his gear, placing the medical kit atop a nearby blue plastic barrel, then unrolling the bedding behind the open gate of the stall. Because the equipment to hoist a downed horse required a minimum of nine feet in clearance, they'd had to rig it from the stable's central beam, which meant Soldier actually stood, supported by the sling, partially outside his stall. Stark placed the air mattress on the ground under the sleeping bag and attached the foot pump that would inflate the coils. Then he rose and turned to face Meredith, his arms folded.

She lifted her worried blue gaze, and asked, "What happens if he develops pneumonia?"

Stark shoved a hand through his hair. "I don't want to give you false hope. Pneumonia can be fatal, especially in an older horse, even one that isn't already seriously ill. Let's just take it a day at a time."

Her chin shot up, and she went on the attack. "False hope! Is that your way of saying you're going to let him die?"

Stark rolled his eyes. "The cat again. And keep your voice down. Animals don't like shouting."

She glanced in the direction of the horses. "Admit it! Your solution for every seriously ill or injured animal is a swift death sentence," she hissed.

He sighed and grated out, "How many times do I have to say it? Your cat was gravely injured. There was nothing I could do."

"You forget," she reminded him tartly,

"that I'm a nurse, and I know something about medical matters."

"For humans," he retorted. "Animals are not people. I suggest that you not assign human attributes to them."

She stepped back as if stung. "I do no such thing!"

"Of course you don't. Which is why your family calls you the crazy cat lady."

"They do not."

"No?" he shot back. "Then why did Ann forbid me to tell you that Donovan's cat had kittens?"

Meredith's eyes lit. "Kittens?"

"*And* I just told you," Stark moaned, pinching the bridge of his nose, suddenly aware of the horses grunting and knocking about in their stalls. "Look, Meredith, I'm sorry about your cat. I'd have saved it if it could have been saved. You can trust me to do all that can be done for every one of my patients."

Meredith adopted a lofty tone, saying, "My concern here is my father's well-being. He's ill, and he loves his horse. I don't want him to suffer any unnecessary losses, not with these tests coming up to determine the status of his cancer. I mean, if that doesn't go well…" She shook her head. "He's been through enough."

Moving his hand to the horse's flank, Stark

stepped closer. It had been a long time since he'd noticed a woman, and he didn't want to notice this one, but those soft blue eyes were tough to ignore. Package them in an oval face with broad, full lips and a petite nose, framed by long, strawberry blond hair, add a shapely figure meant for jeans and knit tops, and he'd dare any man to find a complaint with her looks. Okay, she could be taller. She had to be a foot shorter than him. And she had yet to smile in his presence.

Frowning at that thought, he said, "Meredith, everyone suffers unnecessary loss."

She blinked at him, her head tilting just so, and he knew instantly that he'd given himself away.

Mumbling, "Excuse me," he turned and strode down the aisle of the darkened stable toward the open door and the safety of solitude.

Meredith took a last look at her father's drooping horse before turning and slowly following Stark down the aisle of the stable. As she stepped into the night, she pulled her cardigan closed against the crispness of the mid-October evening and headed toward the welcoming lights of the two-story ranch house across the red-dirt road. As she walked, she prayed for her father and his horse. Stepping up onto the porch, she wondered what "unnecessary loss" Stark Burns had suffered, for she had heard the unmistakable tone of experience in his voice.

That thought and others kept her awake late into the night. She didn't know what came over her when Stark Burns was around. He never frightened her like some men did now, but something about him just pushed her buttons, every last one of them. Even with her cat, Tiger, curled next to her on the narrow bed, Meri couldn't seem to sleep for more than moments at a time. Nevertheless, she woke early the next morning and instantly decided that she owed Stark some sort of apology.

Quickly dressed in jeans, boots and a sweater, she twisted her long, light red hair into a messy bun at the nape of her neck as she left her room. She headed for the stairs, where she met her sister-in-law. Callie held a fingertip to her lips, indicating that at least little Bodie still slept. Wondering if Burns would be awake, Meri slipped out of the house and crossed the road to the stable. He hadn't closed the door, so she crept inside quietly, only to find the light on at the far end of the aisle and the doctor changing an IV bag.

"How is he?" she asked, walking onto the scene.

Burns didn't even spare her a glance. "He's still with us. The next few days will be critical, though."

"What do we do?"

"We keep as close an eye on him as possible, administer fluids and medication, try to get him to eat... I'm monitoring his temperature. That's the important thing right now."

"I can stay with him so you can go to the house for breakfast," she offered politely. "Callie should be cooking as we speak." He shook his head.

"No, thanks. I prefer to take my meals alone."

Meri's mouth fell open. "Always?"

"Usually."

She didn't know what to say to that.

"I have another appointment in an hour so," he went on absently. "I'll get something to eat after that."

We'll see about that, Meredith thought. Wouldn't the confounded man even let her be nice to him?

She turned around and marched straight back to the house, where she found Callie busy in the kitchen, as predicted. Explaining that the doctor had to leave soon for another appointment, Meri quickly loaded up a tray and returned to the stable with her peace offering.

She set the tray, a clean dishcloth draped over it, next to his kit on the blue barrel. Stark sat atop a wooden box and glanced at the tray.

"What's this?"

"Your breakfast. Callie made pancakes and bacon. There's coffee, too, and it's getting cold. How do you take it?"

He frowned at her for a long moment before saying, "Black."

She picked up the mug and held it out to him. "Here you go."

He took the mug, sniffed, sipped, then slugged back a healthy gulp, sighing. "Why does coffee taste so good when you're hungry?"

"I drink it, but I've never much learned to appreciate it," she admitted.

"Why do you drink it, then?" he asked, after swallowing another mouthful.

"Two words," she answered. "Shift work."

"That's right. Nurses work around the clock in shifts."

"And caffeine and shift work go hand in hand."

"I hear you." He set the mug back on the

tray, picked up the whole thing and brought it down to his lap. Balancing the tray on his knees, he slathered butter on the pancakes with the tines of his fork, then poured on the syrup, saying, "This is mighty nice. Of Callie."

Meri rolled her eyes. "You don't give an inch, do you?"

He squinted up at her. "Don't know what you're talking about."

"Really?"

"You going to stand there and watch me eat?" he muttered, stuffing pancake into his mouth.

She turned away. Okay, if he didn't want an apology, she wouldn't give him one. Instead, she moved to the horse, reaching out a hand to signal her presence. Trailing her fingertips over the butternut hide, now dull with illness, she crooned to the animal.

"Hey, boy. How ya doin'?" The horse blew through his nostrils, as if acknowledging her concern, and Meri smiled. "You need to get well. The Straight Arrow wouldn't be the same without you."

"That horse doesn't understand anything but your tone," Stark pointed out laconically. "You know that, right?"

"Do you always have to be so surly?" she

asked, turning just in time to spy a yellow-on-gold-striped cat slink around the bottom of the blue barrel. "Tiger!" she gasped, starting forward, "How did you get out?"

Following her horrified gaze, Stark set the tray aside and slid to the floor, easily capturing the cat as it attempted to streak past him. Crossing his legs at the ankles and bending them at the knees, he brought the cat into his lap, scratching it under the chin.

"Well, well. Haven't seen this guy before. Tiger, is it?" He held up the cat in one hand, checking its eyes, nostrils and teeth with the other. "Healthy fellow."

"I don't know how he got out," Meredith said, fighting the urge to snatch Tiger out of Stark's grasp. "I keep him in my room."

The doctor checked the animal's paws and inclined his head. "Well, a declawed cat shouldn't be out-of-doors, especially not in the country, but a bedroom seems like a small space to keep a cat in."

"It's not permanent," she snapped. "He's usually in my apartment in Oklahoma City. And he was a lot more content before Tux…"

Stark glared at her but otherwise ignored the truncated comment. "Why don't you give him the run of the house? Just keep him out of your dad's room. Contrary to myth, clean animals do not spread contagion."

"I know that. It's just that everybody forgets, and they let him out."

"Poor kitty," Stark cooed, bringing Tiger nose to nose with him. "Nobody looking out for you."

"I look out for him!" Meredith protested hotly. "He's all I have now."

Stark sent her a glance of pure censure, a silent scold that spoke louder than words. She hadn't meant it, of course. She had her whole family, a growing family, which she seemed doomed to leave. And what right did he, a loner by choice, have to judge her, anyway?

Thankfully, Ann called her name just then. Otherwise, she—the quietest, smallest, youngest, mildest, most timid of the Billings siblings—might have been tempted to do Stark Burns harm. Real physical harm.

Chapter Two

"Meri? Meri, the cat's out!"

"We've got him," Meredith called, keeping her voice even. Stark had to admit, if only to himself, that he liked baiting her.

Ann showed up an instant later, breathless, her long, bright hair billowing about her shoulders as she strode confidently down the aisle behind the stalls. "Oh, good."

She was an attractive woman, Ann Billings Pryor, but a mite too in-your-face for Stark's taste, not that Ann's little sister didn't have spunk, too. She'd given him what-for since he'd picked up her injured cat off the road out there next to the house the day of her brother's wedding.

At Ann's heels trotted the spotted Australian shepherd, Digger. While Ann and Dean's son, Donovan, was in kindergarten half days, the dog seemed to have attached itself to Ann. Tiger instantly took exception to the dog, bowing his back and hissing.

"Now, now," Stark crooned, soothing the cat.

"I was looking for you," Ann explained to her sister. "I just cracked the door to your room, and the thing darted out. Dean was coming in the house behind me, and the next thing I knew, it was out the front door."

"Really, Ann," Meredith admonished. "How many times do I have to tell you…and with the dog beside you, no less."

What a prissy little thing she was—prissy, pretty, intelligent and entertaining, an unwelcome combination as far as Stark was concerned. He had no interest in developing a connection with any woman. Still, he felt an odd compulsion to mend fences if he could.

"Let's see if we can introduce these two," Stark suggested, holding out a hand and clucking his tongue at the dog. "Come here, Digger. Come on. That's a boy."

The dog trotted over, and Tiger tried to climb Stark's chest using his back claws. When a cat was declawed, only its defensive front claws were removed. Without those, they had only their tiny teeth and speed for protection. Stark held fast to the feline, talking softly. The dog sniffed and snuffled, while the cat hissed and bared its teeth without making much impression.

"Our cats never act like that around Digger," Ann complained. "Of course, most of them are still kittens." She immediately clapped a hand over her mouth.

"I already spilled the beans on that," Stark admitted with a sheepish grin, while Meredith glared at her sister and the dog trotted off to check out the horses, which were shuffling around their stalls in hopes of being let out soon.

Ann stiffened her spine and squared her shoulders, folding her arms. "Meredith," she said sternly, "you cannot have another cat."

"Why not?" Meredith demanded. "Because I'm the crazy cat lady?"

Stark sighed as Ann glared daggers at him. "One or two spoiled cats do not make a crazy cat lady," he said calmly. In point of fact, Meredith Billings was the furthest thing from a crazy cat lady he'd ever seen. And there was that smile at last.

He almost wished he hadn't seen it. She was really quite amazingly lovely without it. With it, she took away his breath. Her teeth blazed white in her oval face, her plump pink lips forming a perfect bow, while her cheeks plumped into creamy apples and her blue eyes sparkled.

Which was more than enough reason to keep his distance.

The timer on his phone tootled, as if reinforcing that fact. Putting his feet on the floor, he rose in one smooth movement, thrust the cat into its owner's arms and shouldered past the two sisters to the horse.

"I'll just remove the IV bag before I go," he said, "and be back as soon as I can."

"I'll be glad to help," Meredith began.

He gave her instructions as he worked. Nothing much could be done, but someone needed to keep an eye on the animal to make sure it didn't take a turn for the worse before Stark could get back to set up another IV bag and administer more medication. Meredith watched as he removed the connections, leaving the catheter in the jugular.

"I'll make sure Rex knows, and I'll be out here every moment that Dad doesn't need me."

"Dean and I will be here as much as possible, too," Ann promised.

Stark wrapped a bandage loosely around the catheter. "If his breathing seems labored, call me. I'll drop what I'm doing and come."

"Thank you," Meredith whispered, looking worried.

Stark squeezed past her and picked up his kit, intending to walk out, but for some reason he couldn't. He turned to face them, searching for some comfort to offer.

"Seems to be a law of nature," he finally said, "that the crisis comes in the wee hours. I'll be on hand."

"We'll be keeping watch on him all day," Meredith said, stroking her cat.

He knew in his gut that meant *she* would be keeping watch. What he didn't know was why that tied his stomach in knots. He didn't have time to worry about it, though.

As usual, he had a full day of appointments, most of them in the field. Rushing to and from one ranch, farm or homestead, he managed to work in an IV bag for Soldier then return to remove it. Meredith was on hand both times.

By nightfall he'd put nearly 200 miles on his truck and missed lunch, so he'd swung by the diner on his way out to the Straight Arrow. He needed a shower, a shave and a change of clothes, but he couldn't imagine when he'd have found the time. Seeing Meredith trying to coax Soldier to do more than hang his nose over a bucket of nutritional mash came as no surprise. As he walked down the aisle of the stable, the sick horse pushed his broad forehead against her chest. After a moment, she wrapped her arms around the horse, bending her own head to the animal's neck, essentially hugging him, before scooping up a handful of the grainy glop in the pail. Soldier lipped up some of the mash.

The sight did strange things to Stark's chest, things he didn't even want to think about, and that made his voice sharper than he intended.

"You been feeding him by hand all day?"

She nodded defensively. "It's the only way he'll eat."

"Has he taken any water?"

"A little."

Stark laid his kit on the barrel and took off his hat, hanging it on the corner of the stall gate. "Well, he's on IV fluids. But he needs to up his intake if he's going to beat this. Is there anything special he likes to eat?"

"I don't know. I'll ask. He sure doesn't seem to care for that mash of yours."

Her phone dinged. She slipped it from her hip pocket with her clean hand and swiped her thumb over the screen. "Speaking of eating, Rex says we should come in. Dinner's on the table."

Stark held up the paper bag in his left hand. "Brought my own."

Meredith frowned at him. "You must know Callie expected to feed you."

"I'm not here to eat. I'm here to take care of your horse," he retorted, turning his back to unzip his kit.

"How come you make it so hard to be nice to you?" she demanded.

"How come you make it so hard for me to do my job?" he shot back.

"We're just trying to help."

"And I appreciate it, but this is what I do." He turned to face her, holding up the IV bag and moving toward the pole.

"Don't you ever make time to see your friends and family?" she asked, backing up a step.

"I see my friends all the time," he said, hanging the bag. "On the job."

"What about your family?"

Exasperated, he glared at her. "Aren't you supposed to be eating dinner? Or would you rather keep me from mine?"

Huffing, she grabbed a rag from the corner of the stall and scrubbed her hand, muttering, "Why do I even try?"

She slid by him and stalked off down the aisle, only to halt after several steps and pivot on her heel, bringing her hands to her narrow waist.

"Just so you know," she told him smartly, "while I'm praying for my dad and his horse, I'm going to be praying for a wholesale change in your lousy attitude."

"Don't bother," Stark snapped over his shoulder. He turned back to his task, mumbling, "God forgot I existed a long time ago."

He felt her shock and her stare. For a long moment, he expected her to speak again, to demand an explanation or make an argument. Instead, she quietly turned and left him. Grimacing, Stark wished he'd kept his mouth shut. He didn't know why she so easily goaded him into saying too much, but if he wasn't on his guard with her every moment, he found the most surprising things coming out of his mouth.

Sighing, he rubbed the horse's mane, grumbling, "Will you get well so I can get out of here?"

The more distance he could put between himself and Meredith Billings, the better it would be.

Shaking her head, Meredith went into the house and washed up. Sometimes that man made it awfully difficult to be civil to him.

Yet, she couldn't fault his dedication. He'd clearly worked all day, and here he was, ready to take his dinner in a stable and spend the night tending a sick horse. Plus, everyone else in the family thought he was the next thing to perfect, even after she'd told them that he wouldn't be joining them for the meal. As the family bowed their heads over the food, she prayed they were right, at least about his skill as an animal doctor.

Her father's nausea had lessened during the day, and he seemed a little stronger than he had been the day before, but between him and Soldier, she'd had a busy day and suddenly felt quite tired.

Rex spooned the lasagna Callie had made onto his plate, then looked at Meredith and asked, "How's Soldier?"

"I don't know. You'll have to ask Burns. You know, I didn't realize what a sweetheart he is."

"Stark?" Rex asked in obvious surprise.

"No! Soldier. Stark Burns is a grumpy, pigheaded... Well, never mind that."

Rex chuckled. "I think Burns is a better man than you know. As for Soldier, he's always been especially good-natured for a stud."

Meri shook her head. "If you say so. I remember him being frisky and stubborn."

"All studs are that way at first," Rex told her. "Soldier settled down right nice, though. That's why so many of Dad's friends want to breed him. Albright brought some mixed Arabian stock from South America to Texas especially for Soldier. Too bad he brought along a mosquito, too. Even the mosquitos like our Soldier. But at least we get our pick of the colts, and Albright's insurance will cover the vet fees. He'll keep any fillies and remaining colts, so it's still not a bad deal."

"And we get another stud," Meri said.

"That's the plan."

Meredith smiled. "I hope he looks like Soldier."

"He is a fine-looking animal," Rex agreed. "A little Soldier look-alike might soothe Dad if the worst happens." Rex shook his head as if to clear away the gloom and dived into his food. After chewing and swallowing, he said, "I don't know how Stark keeps up the pace. He's planning to spend the night again, isn't he?"

"I assume so."

"How he manages his practice all on his own, I'll never know. That man's busier than a whole litter of hunting dogs."

"Why doesn't he have help?" Meredith wondered aloud.

"I've wondered that myself," Callie put in, setting a big dish of banana pudding on the table. "He's obviously very successful."

"Ooh, my favorite," Rex said, pulling Callie down for a kiss.

Callie chuckled. "You say that about every dessert I serve you."

"I was talking about you."

Meredith sighed mentally, telling herself that it was unbecoming to envy one's siblings. Still, it hurt to feel so...alone. Callie pulled away from Rex and finally took a seat at the table.

"Meri, do you think Wes could manage a bowl of pudding?"

"I think so," Meredith answered. "I'll take some to him in a minute."

She quickly finished her meal, filled a small bowl with banana pudding and carried it into her father's room. He sat in his hospital bed, watching television.

"Hi, sugar. What you got there?"

"Sugar," she quipped. "Callie made banana pudding."

"Yum." He clapped a hand to his flat middle. "Sounds good. I hope it's still warm."

"It is." She handed over the bowl and a spoon.

Wes scooped up the first bite, humming

his approval. With the second bite, he said calmly, "When are you kids going to tell me what's going on?"

Meredith's gaze shot to his. She bit her lip, half-a-dozen options rolling through her mind, but she wasn't about to lie to her father. Not telling him troubling news was one thing, lying to him was something else. On the other hand, this wasn't her decision alone. She walked to the door and stepped out into the hall, calling for her brother. Rex came right away, wiping his mouth with a napkin.

"What's up?"

"The jig," Meri said grimly.

"I'm not deaf," Wes said, "and I keep hearing Stark's name, along with Soldier's."

Rex sighed and gave him an abridged version of the facts, leaving out the detail that they'd found Soldier down in his stall.

Grimacing, Wes set aside his pudding. "And you're sure it's encephalitis?"

"Yes. But Stark's doing all he can," Rex said.

Wes nodded. "I don't doubt it." He glanced at Meredith, adding, "You don't give him enough credit. I've never known a better animal doctor than Stark Burns. I haven't seen many people doctors better than him. And I've had my share of both." Meredith couldn't argue with that. Wes handed the bowl of pudding back to her. "Think I've lost my appetite."

He reached over to his bedside table and picked up his Bible, opening it to Philippians. She knew exactly where he was going. They'd traveled this familiar ground together quite often lately, whenever it was necessary to turn off troublesome thoughts. She'd read the familiar verse to him so often—or vice versa—that she had it memorized.

"Finally, brothers and sisters, whatever is true, whatever is noble, whatever is right, whatever is pure, whatever is lovely, whatever is admirable—if anything is excellent or praiseworthy—think about such things."

A job. Staying close to her family, especially her dad, not slinking away in petulant envy. That was noble, right, admirable. Wasn't it?

She wondered suddenly why Stark Burns didn't have help with his practice. Maybe he couldn't find anyone willing to put up with his special brand of obnoxiousness. Or maybe he just hadn't found anyone with enough experience to be of use to him.

Hmm.

It was worth a shot. If he hired her, she

might even be able to bring a little real compassion to his practice.

She blew a kiss to her dad and left him talking to Rex, then went out to fill another bowl with pudding. Draping a napkin over it, she took a spoon and slipped out to the stable.

Burns was nowhere to be seen—until she drew closer and looked over the stall gate. He reclined on his camp bed, fully clothed, reading on a handheld device.

"Come to check on the horse or badger me?" he asked without so much as glancing in her direction.

She ignored her spiking temper—really, no one else did that to her—and held out the bowl. "I brought you some dessert."

He sent her a dark look, switched off the device and got up to ease past the end of the gate.

"That smells like banana pudding," he said, carefully reaching for the bowl.

"It is."

He made a face.

"Don't you like it?"

"Love it."

She laughed. "Sorry to have pleased you."

Ignoring that, he gingerly took the spoon, crossed to the toolbox, sat and began to eat.

"Good, huh?"

"Very." He continued to eat for several minutes, while she petted the horse and looked around. Suddenly he said, "What do you want, Meredith?"

She tried not to jump at the deep, dark timber of his voice. "I, uh, want to help. In any way that I can."

He said nothing to that, just set aside the empty bowl and spoon. She examined the IV setup carefully from the suspension hook to the catheter, just as if she hadn't already done so repeatedly.

"Very neat job of stitching," she commented. "Do you always stitch the catheter in place?" She didn't think he would answer at first, but eventually he did.

"Even the smartest animals will instinctively pull out something sticking in their bodies, either intentionally or accidentally. Soldier might be too sick now to even realize it's there, but as soon as he's better, he'll try to get rid of it. Can't let that happen. And there's always the chance someone messing around with him will accidentally pull it out."

She shot him a dry look. "I'm the last person you have to worry about doing that."

"Just saying."

"And I'm just saying that I could be of real

help to you if you'd trust me and show me what you need."

"Is that right?"

"I'd go so far as to say that I could help out with a lot of things if you'd let me," Meredith told him cautiously, thinking that had gone easier than she'd expected.

He folded his arms. "Ever seen a calf caught in barbed wire for so long that gangrene has set in?"

She blinked, caught off guard by the change of subject. Then she saw the quirk of his lips just before he swiped the napkin over them, and she knew instantly what he was doing.

Parking her hands at her waist, she said, "No. But I've seen plenty that would turn your stomach."

They traded horror stories for several minutes, each more gory than the last.

Laughter bubbled up inside of her when she finally called a halt. "Look, I'm a nurse. You can't gross me out."

A grin split his tanned face. "Okay. Okay. Truce?"

She nodded. "Truce."

"And thank you for the pudding," he said, picking up the empty bowl and spoon.

Well, that was progress. She took a deep breath and plunged in.

"I was wondering…hoping you might need help with your practice."

Sobering, he looked down. "No."

Just like that? "But Rex says that you work alone and that your practice is huge, too big for one person."

"Meredith," he said, "I *prefer* to work alone."

Her heart sank. Could he be that antisocial? "Truly?"

Shoving up to his feet, he held out the spoon and bowl, nodding. "That's how I like it."

"But why? Everyone says you have too much to do."

"That's true," he admitted. "Still, I prefer to work alone."

"That makes no sense."

"Why would you want a job with me, anyway?" he asked, not even denying her last statement. "You're an RN."

"In case you haven't noticed," she retorted, snatching the bowl from his hand hard enough to rattle the spoon, "there aren't any nursing jobs around here. I've checked. I've put my name on the lists at all the hospitals and nursing homes within driving distance, and I've registered with every local agency.

I've even called every doctor I can find. No one's hiring."

"I'm sorry," he said. "What happened to your job in the City? I'm sure Rex told me you were taking a leave of absence."

"It's still there," she admitted glumly. "But I don't want to go back. I want to be *here*. I've always wanted to be here. Not at the ranch, necessarily, but in War Bonnet or close to. And now that Rex and Ann have come home to stay…" She shook her head.

"Just because they've come home doesn't mean you have to," he pointed out.

"You aren't listening. I never wanted to be in the City. You've no idea how much I hate it there. I want to come home. I want to be close to my family. I wasn't really close to Dad growing up, and now it's like we have a second chance. I want to be *here*."

"I want lots of things I'll never have again, Meredith," he said softly. "I'm sorry, but I can't help you."

Struggling not to weep, she shrugged, nodded and whispered, "Well, I have some time yet. Something might turn up."

"You never know," he said.

But she did know, all too well, and his tone said that he did, too. The truth was that if he didn't give her a job, she wasn't going to find one locally. The worst part was that it didn't make sense. She could help Stark. They could help each other.

Why wouldn't he take what she offered?

Did he dislike her that much?

Or was something else going on here?

Either way, unless God intervened, she was on her way back to Oklahoma City. Like it or not.

Chapter Three

As tired as he was, Stark had a difficult time dropping off to sleep between the hourly alarms set on his phone. He'd been too long without rest and knew his judgment would be impaired without it, but he couldn't get Meredith Billings out of his mind. If she'd been male or fifty or as ugly as a mud fence, he'd have hired her with gratitude last night, but he had no room in his life, such as it was, for a pretty little thing like her.

No, the last thing he needed underfoot was an attractive female like Meri. He couldn't afford to take a chance that one or the other of them might form an attachment. After losing Cathy, he was never going there again. He'd never survive a second loss like that. Truthfully, he hadn't really survived the first one. All that was left of him was an empty husk and the work. He tried to concentrate on the latter and ignore everything else.

The horse seemed unchanged when Stark checked around four in the morning. He considered belting back one of the energy drinks that he lived on but decided against it. Instead, he stretched out on his bedroll again. The next thing he knew a woman's shrieking voice woke him.

"Stark! He's not breathing! Stark!"

The smell of strong black coffee cut through the odors of the stable, but he didn't have time to think about it as he all but vaulted the stable gate. Meredith stood at Soldier's head, her expression one of sheer horror. The horse's head hung almost to the floor. Only the sling kept the animal upright. Stark grabbed his kit and found his stethoscope. After a quick examination, he was able to think.

"His heart's still beating, but I don't know how long he's been without oxygen." Stark began palpating the horse's windpipe and giving orders. "Quick. I need a trach kit. Right side of the bag. And lay out a sterile sheet. Blue."

Kneeling in the stall, Meredith worked swiftly, pulling on gloves and following instructions to the letter while Stark suited up. They had the tube in place in less than two minutes. Immediately Soldier twitched his ears and rasped in air. Holding the tracheotomy tube with one hand, Stark reached up to mop his brow with the other wrist, but Meredith beat him to it, blotting his forehead with a gauze pad. When he looked down, she had the suture kit open. As soon as he picked up the curved needle with the sewing silk threaded through it, she squirted antiseptic around the incision holding the breathing tube. It was as if the woman could read his mind.

Working quickly, Stark secured the breathing tube, while a lightly sedated Soldier swayed on his hooves, occasionally flicking his ears. Finally, Stark stepped back, satisfied with the work and the result.

He peeled off his gloves and tore off the coverall, saying grimly, "Get your brother while I clean up." Shucking her gloves, Meredith dropped them onto the blue plastic sheet. "Meri," he said, as she edged past him. She paused. It cost him, but he had to say it. "Good work." She shot him a smile. "That doesn't mean he's out of the woods," he warned.

Nodding soberly, she took off at a trot. Stark used the stethoscope once more, listening to the faint rattle in Soldier's lungs.

By the time Meredith returned to the stable with Rex, Stark had bundled up the detritus from the tracheotomy and deposited it in the trash. He'd also zipped up his kit and performed a more thorough examination of the horse.

"Swelling in the retropharyngeal lymph nodes." He showed Rex the bulging on the undersides of the horse's jaws. "It doesn't always happen with encephalitis, but it's not that unusual."

"So what do we do now?" Meredith asked worriedly.

Stark rubbed his chin, rough with three days' growth of beard. Meredith had been a great help. She'd kept a very cool head during what had been a true emergency and had anticipated his every need as he'd worked. He couldn't help being impressed by that. Now he was going to have to count on her to tend the horse while he was away, because he simply could not be in two places at one time. That was a fact with which he often had to deal, but it was seldom more essential than now.

"Basically, we watch him like a hawk," Stark said. "We were sure lucky you woke me when you did."

Almost as one, the brother and sister said, "I don't believe in luck."

That rocked Stark back. "You don't believe in luck?"

"Not a bit of it," Meredith told him firmly. She smiled at her brother, saying, "We believe in divine providence."

Smiling, Rex wrapped an arm around his little sister's shoulders and hugged her. "I thank God you walked in when you did."

Stark clamped his jaw. He was well aware of the Christian teaching of divine providence, but he didn't believe it for a moment. To believe that God tended to the personal lives of the average person was to believe that God had allowed Stark's family to die, and *that* Stark could not—would not—accept.

He licked his lips and said, "Be that as it may, we're working with a heap of negatives here. Encephalitis. Lymph node inflammation severe enough to cut off the air passage. And, from the sound of his breathing, pneumonia."

"Oh, no," Rex said, pushing a hand over his face.

"So that's it?" Meredith demanded pugnaciously, parking her hands at her waist, and quite a neat little waist it was, too. In fact, she curved nicely in all the right places, which just made Stark want to run right out of there. "You're going to recommend putting him down, aren't you?"

Stark was trying so hard not to look at her that he almost didn't hear her. When her words finally registered, he welcomed them and the anger that they stirred. "No, Miss High-and-Mighty. I have to admit that his chances have diminished, but I'm not ready to give up on him yet. Are you?"

"Of course not," she retorted, sounding both relieved and affronted.

"Good. Then you won't mind babysitting him while I'm gone." Stark reached down and snatched up his kit.

"H-how long will you be away?" she asked.

"I don't know," he all but snarled, shouldering the kit. The woman sure had a way of getting under his skin. He took a deep breath. "It depends on how many other patients I have." He pulled two syringes from his shirt pocket and held them out to her. "One in the IV plug every four hours. There's an extra IV bag next to my bedroll. Change it out when this one is down to the last mark. These big bags are tricky to estimate, so pull the bottom out like this to make sure how much is in it." He demonstrated with both hands. "Watch the flow rate. If it dumps too fast, it'll wash out all the medication, so check periodically."

Meredith nodded. "Got it."

"Don't try to feed or water him today. If he starts to struggle, coughs or collapses, call me *at once*. Think you can handle all that?"

"Yes. Absolutely."

"I hope so, because the alternative is to try to get him to a clinic, and, frankly, I doubt he'd survive the trip."

She looked stricken at that.

Rex said, "I don't think we should tell Dad just how bad it is. Not yet."

Meredith nodded, then looked at Stark as if asking for his input. The very idea made him break out in gooseflesh. He shook his head.

"None of my business. I take care of the horse. Wes is your father. Y'all take care of him."

She looked to her brother, saying, "Whatever you think best."

Those words slugged Stark in the chest, echoing down through the years.

Whatever you think best, sweetheart. We'll leave whenever you're ready.

Stark practically ran after that, getting out of there as fast as he could. No matter how hard he tried, though, he couldn't escape the memories. Throwing his gear into his truck, he all but dove behind the wheel. Then he sat there for several long minutes, shuddering at the sounds in his mind of screeching tires and clanging metal. When at last the empty silence returned, he started the truck and, with shaking hands, went doggedly on his way. His lonely, tortured way.

"I'm sorry," Dean argued quietly the next evening, his handsome blond head shaking. "I think you're wrong." A custom farmer, he'd come straight from the harvest to make his case, having neither showered nor eaten, so strongly did he feel. The weather forecast hinted at rain, which made for a long day for the harvesters. "When my granddad was ill, I learned quick that he resented more than anything for me and Grandma to try to protect him," Dean said. "Grandpa said it robbed him of his pride and his manhood. Even though he was dying, I learned that the best thing I could do was sit down and talk man-to-man with him about whatever problems we were having."

"And you were, what," Ann asked, sitting beside him on the porch swing, "all of fifteen? Those must've been tough times for you, darling." She brushed dust from his knee.

He nodded, wrapping his hand around hers. "They were. Now I have every hope that Wes is going to recover, but I'm not sure he'll be happy if you keep this from him."

"I have to agree," Ann said, but then she was so in love with her husband that he could say the moon was made of seaweed and she would at least try to believe it.

Rex leaned against the porch railing, folding his arms. They'd convened this little family conference on the porch in order to be well out of Wes's hearing, but they were still keeping their voices low. As he had recently proved, Wes was far from deaf.

"Dad's so weak," Rex mused, "and he loves that old horse. I—I just don't know if we should tell him how serious the situation is. I feel we need to give Dad as much incentive as we can to live right now."

"Maybe we could wait a day or two," Callie suggested, sliding an arm around Rex's waist.

Somewhere in the dark, an owl hooted. It was such a lonely sound, exactly how Meredith felt, standing here surrounded on a moonless October night by her siblings and their spouses. Still, it was better than sitting locked in her apartment with only her cat for company.

"Maybe Dr. Burns can give us some insight," she said.

"Why don't you go ask him?" Ann suggested.

Meredith caught—and ignored—the slightly suggestive undertone in her sister's voice. "All right." She turned away from the house. "He should've had time to make a full assessment of the horse by now."

He had arrived well over an hour earlier, his usual bag from the local diner in tow. At some point during the day, he had taken the time to shower, shave and change clothes. He'd even shown up wearing a different hat, a cleaner, better version of his usual black felt Stetson. The sight had done strange, unwelcome things to her breathing, so she'd scampered out of the stable as quickly as she could, but she wouldn't let that keep her from seeking him out now. She might not like Stark Burns, but he was in no way a danger to her. She knew that, had always known it, by sheer instinct.

Stepping off the porch, she walked down the well-beaten path beneath the trees. Behind her, she heard the thin wail of a tiny voice. Bodie was teething again, and sleep seemed to be eluding her. Meredith heard the screen door creak as her sister-in-law went into the house to see to the child. Ann and Dean had left Donovan at home with Dean's grandmother.

Meri heard Ann say, "We ought to be getting back. Dean's tired. Call me later."

Rex replied something to that, but Meredith couldn't make it out as she was moving farther from the house. She hopped over the bar ditch and out onto the dirt road. The vapor lamp atop the pole at the edge of the big red barn cast a wide circle of faint light over Stark's truck. Cream colored, it looked gray in the light. The magnetic sign on its door read, Burns Veterinary Services, with a phone number beneath, followed by the words, War Bonnet, Oklahoma. He hadn't bothered to include an address. War Bonnet was so small that a short drive around town would quickly locate the veterinary office on its outskirts, just past the Feed & Grain owned by Callie's father.

Walking past the truck, Meredith stepped out of the circle of dim light and into the darkness once more before crossing the second bar ditch on the opposite side of the road, then crawling through the corral fence. There was a gate, but no one used it except to let horses in or out or drive truckloads of feed inside. As usual, except in the very coldest part of winter, the stable door stood open.

Meredith walked through the door and knew at once that Stark wasn't inside.

She had no idea why he'd stepped out, but obviously he had. He couldn't have gone far, though. His truck was still parked at the side of the road.

Going to Soldier, she checked his tracheotomy then the IV, the catheter first, followed by the bag. Wanting an accurate measurement, she tried to do it just the way Stark had shown her, pulling on the bottom of the big, heavy bag.

Suddenly, two arms came around her, trapping her, and two hands covered hers. Meredith screamed and jerked backward, colliding with a warm, strong body. Panicked, she threw first one elbow then the other and tore free, stumbling into the stall and throwing up her hands in defense.

"No! Let go! I'll fight!"

Stark stood there, his arms held up, hands shoulder high and spread wide. "It's okay," he said gently.

Meri's heart pounded so hard she thought she might be sick. Clasping a hand over the scar on her chest, she doubled over, gasping and swallowing down air.

"I thought you knew I was there," he told her evenly, rubbing his ribs. "I just stepped out to enjoy the cool air for a minute. I followed you in. Didn't mean to surprise you."

She tried to stop shaking, memories of the assault flashing over her, a dark night, a quiet place... She heard his voice telling her to shut up and do as she was told, saw the knife flash, felt it slice into her flesh. He'd dragged her backward between two cars.

"I..." Not another word would come.

"I was just going to correct your hand position," Stark said conversationally, reaching for the bag. "You need to pull on the tabs. Like this." He demonstrated how to properly get a measurement of the liquid left in the bag.

Meredith glanced over at him and nodded, gulping down air to settle her stomach. "I'm sorry," she finally managed.

"For what?" he asked. "You didn't scare me. I scared you. I should apologize." Very sincerely, his hand placed flat against the center of his chest, he said, "I'm sorry."

She knew that he was apologizing for more than scaring her, for something that he had not even done. Tears filled her eyes. She shook her head, waved a hand, tried to make light of it.

"It was silly."

But it wasn't silly. It would never be silly. She pushed it down, closed it off, as she had done from the beginning, and tilted her chin at the horse.

"How is he?"

"I feel he's improved," Stark said, easily shifting subjects. "I can't quantify that, mind you. Just a feeling I have."

Blowing out a breath, Meredith tried to smile, to feel better. It didn't work. Fear had its claws in her now, and she knew from experience that it would be slow to let go.

"That's..." She tried to swallow the knot strangling her. "That's good. W-we have to decide what to tell Dad. Ann and Dean think he'll resent being kept in the dark, but Rex and I don't want to worry him unnecessarily."

Stark shrugged. "None of my business either way, but I'll happily talk to Wes if it'll help."

"All right. Thanks. I'll let you know."

She looked toward the door and the darkness beyond, suddenly dreading what now seemed like a long and very frightening walk back to the house. Gulping down the lump in her throat, she sucked in a deep breath, squared her shoulders and prepared to say that she would leave. He beat her to it.

"I need to get something from my truck," he announced. "If you're ready, I'll, uh, walk you out."

He knew. He knew she was frightened. And at least suspected why. A sliver of the old shame pricked her, but she was too glad of the escort to pay it much mind at the moment.

Push it down. Pack it away. Think of other things.

Whatever is true, whatever is noble, whatever is right, whatever is pure, whatever is lovely, whatever is admirable...

Nodding, she clasped her hands together and walked as casually as she could manage out into the aisle of the stable. He fell into step beside her, his hands tucked into the back pockets of his jeans.

As they reached the door, he said, "You've really been a lot of help."

She felt herself relax incrementally. "That's nice to hear."

To her surprise, he turned to the right, taking a path that would carry them behind the stable, rather than to the left, the shorter path.

"I go this way," he said, "because of the light."

It was true that the vapor light shined over here. She hadn't thought of it before, always choosing the shorter path, but then she hadn't been frightened until now. Silently she trailed along in his wake. He climbed the fence. She crawled through. He didn't try to help her, just waited for her to reach the other side. They crossed the bar ditch. She leaped, but it was hardly out of stride for him. As they walked over the dirt road, he didn't even look at his truck, just moved on toward the house.

"I was wondering what sort of hours you were looking for," he said. "In a job, I mean."

Meredith caught her breath and had to focus to keep from stumbling. "I'm adaptable," she answered carefully. "I'm used to shift work, after all."

"Mmm. And pay? Nurses make good wages, better than you're likely to find around here."

"Well, I wouldn't have to pay rent," she said quickly, "or utilities or even buy groceries, if I don't want to. And gasoline is certainly cheaper, not to mention insurance, and then there's fees. You've no idea how many fees are involved in nursing. So I could settle for less than I'm used to."

"Uh-huh. Anything else in particular you're looking for?"

"It'd be nice if I could wear scrubs, at least initially." She wrinkled her nose, admitting, "I really don't have that many clothes anymore. I mean, where would I wear them? It's not like I go out. I work. I go to church when I can. That's it." Embarrassed, she looked down at her boots, realizing only then that they'd come to a halt on the pathway beneath the trees.

"There'd be a learning curve, you know."

Meredith looked up, elated. So he really was thinking about hiring her. "I understand, but I'm a fast learner, and I love animals. I really do."

"That might not be as much of a plus as you think." He strolled onward. "Animals can't tell us where or how it hurts, but they do suffer, and when they suffer, it's obvious."

"I understand," she told him softly.

"Do you? They suffer, Meri, and sometimes they die. And too often there's nothing we can do about it. That's just the fact of it."

They had reached the house. She lifted a hand to the porch column, looking up at him. "Why do you try to discourage me?"

"Why do you want it so badly?" he countered. "You don't even like me. Doesn't make sense that you want to work for me."

She could have lied to him, could've batted her lashes and even flirted a little, but that wasn't her way.

"I may not always like you," she said bluntly,

"but I have come to respect you. And you're my only option." She ducked her head, adding softly, "I've never felt safe there. I've never been happy there. I don't want to go back."

He said nothing for a long while. Then, when she looked up, he abruptly glanced away.

"I'll think on it," he told her, stepping away from her.

Meredith smiled, turned, climbed up onto the porch and went into the house. He'd given her hope at least.

Tonight had shown her that she couldn't go back. She just couldn't.

She'd thought she was past it. After all the counseling and all the precautions, she'd held on there as long as anyone could possibly expect. In the back of her mind, she'd thought that this respite, this sojourn at home, would at least prepare her to return to the City and her work there, but it had done the opposite. Her time here had shown her that she could never go back. She should be free now to find peace and safety. At home.

Please, God. She just wanted to come home to stay.

Chapter Four

Melting into the shadows, Stark watched Meredith enter the house. No wonder she was so desperate to find a job and stay here. He recognized all the signs of trauma now that he'd bothered to look. He ought to—he dealt with them himself pretty much on a daily basis. Oh, he didn't scream at the unexpected touch of another's hands, but sometimes when he passed a tractor-trailer rig on the highway… He shuddered, trying not to remember.

All too often he woke in the night, struggling to free himself from the twisted metal, calling the names of his wife and daughter. How many times had he asked himself why he hadn't left earlier? Or later? Just ten minutes would have made all the difference.

Whatever you think best, sweetheart. We'll leave whenever you're ready.

Meredith's trauma didn't stem from a freak accident, however. Her terror had been personal, deep, real and instantaneous. The moment he'd put his hands on her, the panic had completely overtaken her. She'd flashed back to some terrifying, horrifying event, and he very much feared that he knew what it was.

The thought made him ill. If he was right, and his gut told him that he very well could be, he wouldn't have to worry about her developing an interest in him—or likely any other man—anytime soon. No wonder she didn't like him. Not that he'd given her any reason to.

He wondered how long ago it had happened, who the man was. Surely Rex and Wes knew, but of course he couldn't ask. Stark hoped sincerely that whoever had done that to her was locked away. Permanently.

Not that it was any of his concern. He had enough to deal with already.

Like a practice that was really far too big for one person alone to handle.

He rubbed his hands over his face. Maybe he should hire her and be done with it. She was certainly capable, and he wasn't likely to find anyone else around here to match her skills. It might be the best solution all the way around. The unattainable man hiring the unattainable woman. Perfect.

Except…

Why couldn't *she* have been a *he*? Some gawky kid who wouldn't think twice about Stark's rough ways or where he ate his meals?

Because God hadn't been that good to Stark Burns in a long time, that's why not.

At least that's what Stark told himself as he ambled back out to the stable.

An owl hooted from somewhere near the old red barn. It was a lonely sound.

Loneliness, too, Stark knew well. It never left him, hadn't left him in nearly four long years.

The anniversary of that awful day approached quickly. He tried to ignore it, telling himself that he hadn't even been aware of the moment when his wife and daughter had left this earth, but that didn't help. It only added to his guilt.

Shoving his hands into the pockets of his jeans, he walked back to the stable. The horse switched its tail when Stark drew near. Yes, definite improvement. That didn't mean Soldier would recover, but a good sign was a good sign. He set his alarms and turned in.

His last thought before he slipped into sleep was that Meredith didn't deserve to be frightened. He saw the look of terror on her face, and in his dreams, instead of standing there like a lump, he held out his arms, and she walked into them, smiling tremulously.

Her hair smelled of coconut. He didn't know why or how he knew that, but somehow he woke the next morning with that fragrance in his nostrils.

Cathy had smelled of strawberries. He would never forget. The fragrance of strawberries sometimes still threatened to move him to tears, strawberries and sour apples. Bel had loved a certain tart candy that tasted of sour apples. Sometimes he bought a pack and opened it just to savor the smell, but then he had to throw it away.

What did Meredith Billings do to bring herself comfort?

She was trying to move home. And he could help her with that.

She and her strawberry blond, coconut-scented hair arrived with black coffee and a breakfast tray around six in the morning. He was waiting for her, sitting atop the toolbox.

"Morning."

She gave him that devastating smile along with the breakfast tray. "Good morning."

"Swelling's gone down," he told her, parking the tray on his knees. "I expect to repair the tracheotomy tomorrow."

"That's good."

He removed the dish towel, uncovering a thick omelet topped with salsa and cheese, along with rolled tortillas and sliced melon. The Billings family did not stint in the kitchen. Mouth watering, he picked up his fork and said slowly, "I could use your help."

Meredith caught her breath, but he pretended not to notice.

"Okay," she said. "Someone has to miss service tomorrow to stay with Dad anyway."

He'd forgotten that tomorrow was Sunday. He hated Sundays. They were his slowest days. This particular Sunday he hated most of all. But he wouldn't think about that. He never thought about that.

Right.

Keeping his gaze on his plate, he said, "Best do it early."

"That's fine. After breakfast okay?"

"Works for me."

"That's settled then. Now, I have a favor to ask."

Stark steeled himself, setting aside his fork to slug back strong black coffee, and nodded noncommittally. "You can ask."

"You said you'd talk to Dad, give him an update on Soldier."

Stark relaxed. "No problem."

"We thought you might do that this evening. Ann and Dean are coming over for dinner. We'll tell Dad everything that's been going on the last few days, then you can give him the latest update on Soldier's condition. If that's all right with you."

He knew she was asking him to do more than simply speak to her father about his horse, and he meant to tell her that speaking to Wes was *all* he would do, that he would not join the family for dinner, but he couldn't seem to think of words that weren't too sharp, rude or unintentionally wounding. In the end, he nodded curtly and ate his omelet. It had nothing, nothing whatsoever, to do with the date. Or so he told himself. Smiling, she skipped out of the stable, leaving him frowning at her back.

Looked like he was having dinner with the Billings family.

He tried not to think about it, going about his business on Saturday as usual. Plenty needed to be done. Somehow, though, he still found enough time to shower, shave, change and show up at the stable in time to give Soldier a thorough exam before Meredith insisted on dragging him into the house. She'd changed the IV bag before he'd arrived, and, try as he might, he could find no fault with her work.

"You want me to give your father a comprehensive report, don't you?" he grumbled as she towed him by the arm down the aisle of the stable.

"Yes, and I also want to eat before dinner gets cold."

He rolled his eyes, dragging his feet, but inside he felt an alarming tendency to smile. Countering it with a scowl, he allowed himself to be escorted to the ranch house. As soon as he passed through the front door into the foyer, he removed his hat and hung it on a peg on the wall. The instant he stepped into the living room, however, a little redheaded tornado hurled himself off the couch and straight at Stark.

Instinctively, Stark backed up a step, but the boy lassoed his arms around Stark's legs and squeezed, bellowing, "Hi!"

Throwing up his hands, Stark raised his eyebrows at the boy. "Uh, hi."

Meredith chuckled. "How about me? Don't I get a hug?"

The kid immediately threw himself on her,

encircling her waist with his arms. "Hi, Aunt Meri."

"Hello, Donovan. Want to let Aunt Callie know that Dr. Burns is here?"

The boy ran off, bellowing, "Aunt Callie, Dr. Burns is here!"

Meredith grinned at Stark. "If Donovan sees you twice, you're best friends."

"Uh-huh."

It had been a long while since he'd felt comfortable dealing one-on-one with a child, almost exactly four years, in fact. Doing so made him nervous, and sometimes it actually hurt. He knew too well how fragile children could be, and every little face brought bittersweet feelings and memories. He thought of his little niece, Jeanie Ruth, who was about Donovan's age and looked so like his daughter. Bel had been shy with strangers, but unfailingly polite, speaking in a tiny, husky voice. Once she warmed up, Bel's giggles could fill a room, like soap bubbles, light, sparkling and airy. Jeanie Ruth, on the other hand, was a demanding little tyrant who ruled her world with a petulant iron will. Stark loved her, but he could hardly bear to be around her simply because looking into Jeanie Ruth's face was like looking into his daughter's.

Rex came in behind him and Meredith, entering through the back hall and the foyer. "Y'all come on back to Dad's room. Callie says dinner will be a few minutes yet."

Stark shot Meredith a censorious look, but she put her nose in the air and followed her brother into the foyer and down the hall, past the front and back stairs, skirting the kitchen to the far back hall and the door to Wes's room. Rex had told Stark that, before their deaths, Wes's parents had used this room as their own. Wes had moved into it after his cancer surgery so he wouldn't have to go up and down the stairs to the master bedroom. The door stood open, and Donovan's parents, Ann and Dean Pryor, were already inside. Rex lifted a hand, indicating that both Meredith and Stark should go in ahead of him. Meredith slipped in and took a seat in one of a pair of chairs facing Wes's hospital bed. Stark walked in, followed by Rex. They all kept a good distance from Wes.

"This doesn't look good," Wes rasped, glancing at Stark.

"It could be worse," Stark announced, smiling, "and there has been improvement." He quickly detailed the swollen glands and the emergency tracheotomy, adding, "That's all cleared up now. In fact, Meredith and I will be removing the trach tube tomorrow morning." Wes looked at Meredith with some surprise, compelling Stark to add, "If Meredith hadn't been there that morning, we might have lost Soldier."

Wes beamed at Meredith. "That's my girl."

She grinned broadly. Stark cleared his throat, feeling a strange space open inside his chest.

"The thing is, we still have the encephalitis to get past, and his lungs are rattling. I suspect a touch of pneumonia." Wes lifted a hand to his hairless brow. "There are no guarantees," Stark went on, "but I'm somewhat encouraged. Soldier has rallied quicker than I expected, all things considered, and if I can get him eating after the trach site is healed, he's got a good chance."

Wes nodded and, almost shamefacedly, said, "He loves apples and bananas."

Stark tried not to grin. "We'll add them to the mash then, alternating them so they offset each other."

Wes sighed, then fixed his children with a basilisk glare, demanding, "Anything else I should know? Barn burned down? Cattle all been rustled? Ranch in bankruptcy?"

Rex shook his head. "Everything's fine, Dad. You can't blame us for trying to spare you."

"I'm not in a box waiting for you to throw dirt over me," Wes groused. "Stop treating me like I'm on my deathbed."

Dean coughed behind his fist.

"Oh, stuff it," Rex rumbled from behind a smile. "Nobody likes an I-told-you-so."

"I do," Ann said, stroking her husband's head.

Meredith rolled her eyes at exactly the same time Stark did.

Wes laughed. "Get on out of here, all of you," he ordered good-naturedly. "I'm not used to so much company." As they all filed out, he called, "Dean, you keep them in line now."

Grinning, Dean said, "You can count on me."

Rex poked him in the ribs playfully. "And to think you used to be my favorite brother-in-law."

Grinning, Dean shoved at Rex's hands. "I'm your *only* brother-in-law."

"Yeah, but you're not my favorite any longer," Rex razzed.

"You're just jealous because Dean was right," Ann said in her husband's defense, looping her arms around his neck.

"Even a broken clock is right twice a day," Rex retorted to general laughter.

Stark shook his head at their banter, following the others to the kitchen table. He felt very much like the odd man out. He'd once known times like these, family laughing and teasing, but that was almost painful in its foreignness now.

He moved to the seat at the table pointed out to him, waited until the women were all seated, then dropped down, staring at his lap while Rex prayed in gratitude for the meal. And such a meal it was. Stark hadn't eaten so well in ages. Even with two children at the table, little Bodie in her highchair and freckle-faced Donovan on and off his knees in his chair, Stark was able to ignore those around him and concentrate on the food.

Then, in a lull in the conversation, Ann asked, "What about you, Stark, do you have brothers or sisters?"

He hadn't paid attention to the conversation that had led up to that point, but he swallowed and answered briefly. "One brother, two sisters, all younger."

"Obviously they don't live close by," Meredith surmised.

He shook his head, hoping that would be the end of it, but Rex remarked, "You're originally from Tulsa, aren't you?"

"That's right."

Dean frowned. "I thought it was Ponca City."

Stark turned over his spoon, feeling as if all the air was being sucked out of the room. "I did live in Ponca City before I came here."

"I'm surprised you never married," Callie commented, smiling.

The walls seemed to close in suddenly on him. His heart pounding, Stark tersely said, "I married." Then he picked up his fork and filled his mouth again.

Silence filled the space for several heartbeats. Then Callie apologized softly. "I'm sorry. That was ill-mannered of me."

Stark shook his head and attempted a smile, wondering why he'd thought this had been a good idea. He'd have been better off alone, trying not to think, fighting not to remember. He finished his plate, refused dessert, excused himself, thanked everyone, and got out of there, saying he needed to check on the horse. When his feet hit the red-dirt road between the home place and the outbuildings, he finally caught a good breath again. But what a lonely, cold solace that was. He knew he would not sleep tonight, and tomorrow would come. It always came. Year after lonely, agonizing year.

* * *

Armed with a breakfast tray, determination and small talk, Meredith made her way out to the stable the next morning just as the rest of the family, with the exclusion of her father, headed off to church. Rex, Callie and little Bodie would meet Ann, Dean, Donovan and Dean's grandmother there. For the first time in quite a while, Meredith was not secretly envious of her big brother and sister. Ready, even eager, for work, she'd worn an old pair of green scrubs, faded from many washings, over a long-sleeved white turtleneck and athletic shoes with solid leather toe caps for maximum protection. Her hair was caught at her nape in a thick ponytail and rolled into a bun secured with a heavy spider clip.

Last night's dinner had been enlightening in several ways. For one thing, she hadn't been wrong about Stark's dislike of children. For another, he'd finally let slip some personal information. That he had siblings wasn't exactly earthshaking. The news that he had married at some point had been shocking enough that she had slipped off to the office after he left to do a little research on the computer. What she had found explained a lot about the irascible animal doctor and why today, of all days, he did not need to be alone.

Stark uncovered the plate filled with biscuits, sausage, gravy, scrambled eggs, and hash browns. "Wow," he said, lifting the mug of steaming black coffee. "Your sister-in-law really puts on a feed on Sunday morning."

Actually, Callie did a fairly light breakfast on Sundays. Meredith had added the gravy and hash browns herself, reasoning that both her dad and Stark could use the extra calories just then. She merely smiled, however, and went to pet Soldier, who nosed around her pockets as if looking for a treat.

"He seems hungry."

"Noticed that. We'll have to be careful not to give him too much food or water for a while. Hungry horses don't know when to stop."

While Stark ate, they discussed how long it would be before they could try Soldier on the soft mash again. Eventually Stark changed the subject, remarking that Wes seemed improved.

"Yes, I'm cautiously optimistic," Meredith admitted. "Only time will tell if the cancer is gone, but the early tests were encouraging. Soon, as his immune system grows stronger, he'll be able to join the family at the dinner table again. Gradually he'll be able to get out and about." She left the horse, faced Stark, and said bluntly, "Then my reason for staying on at the ranch will be gone."

Sighing, Stark set aside the now-empty breakfast tray and rose. "Let's get to work."

"That's why I'm here."

He pulled gloves from his kit and thrust them at her before placing a bottle of medication, alcohol wipes and a syringe on the top of the blue barrel. "You can sedate him while I suit up."

As Stark pulled on the protective, sterile paper coveralls, he told her how much medication to inject into which IV port. She administered the medication, then laid out the sterile sheet and necessary equipment to remove the tracheotomy tube and close up the incision, which had to be done on several levels. That meant shaving the area immediately surrounding the tube-insertion site and a great deal of sterilization. Soldier took exception to some of the work, which required Meredith to physically restrain him. Had the animal not been sedated, she'd never have had a chance of keeping him still, but he had enough of the drug in him to keep him relatively docile.

After what seemed like hours to her, Stark

finally stepped back and began peeling off his gloves, saying, "Well, that took less time and effort than I'd expected."

She blinked at him, her tired arms like lead weights at her sides. "Really? That was easy for you?"

He smiled as he tore away the protective garment and added it to the pile of debris on the blue sheet. "Changing your mind about working in veterinary medicine?"

"No," she said quickly. "I'm just always surprised when you admit that I've been of help. Does this mean you'll give me a job?"

He crouched, gathering up the corners of the sheet. She added her gloves to the pile and, fighting the urge to skitter around like a bug on a hot plate, watched him carefully bundle up the detritus.

"Was it that bad?" he asked as he worked, studiously not looking up at her. "What happened to you in the City?"

Her breath caught in her chest. She forced it out again, straightening her suddenly fisted fingers. The scar above her left breast seemed to burn, and her feet itched to run. Shifting her weight, she stood her ground.

"Yes."

Nodding, he rose, the trash bundle grasped in one hand. "I'm sorry."

Unexpectedly, warmth swept through her, bringing an odd comfort. In that moment, she only wanted to offer him the same thing, so she blurted, "I'm sorry, too. About your family."

He stepped back as if she'd struck him. A terrible, heartbreaking kind of horror flashed across his face, followed instantly by a thunderous expression that had *her* stepping back. The next instant he turned and stalked off down the aisle of the stable and out the door.

Meredith clapped a hand over her mouth and bowed her head, swiftly sending up a prayer.

Oh, Lord, forgive me! What have I done?

She hadn't meant to blindside him like that. Stark Burns was a private man, and today was the anniversary of the deaths of his wife and daughter. She'd meant only to help him with his work and keep him company, not drive him away by blurting out facts she wasn't even supposed to know.

The newspaper account she'd read said only that a tractor-trailer rig had too quickly taken a sharply curving highway entrance ramp on the outskirts of Tulsa and turned over, causing a multiple-vehicle pileup and tying up traffic for several hours. The result was three deaths, the driver of the truck and a mother and her daughter, Catherine and Belinda Burns, ages thirty-three and nine, respectively, both of Ponca City, Oklahoma. Husband and father, Dr. Stark Burns, had been hospitalized with non-life-threating injuries, along with several others. Before his death, the driver of the tractor-trailer rig had apologized repeatedly, according to emergency personnel at the scene.

Meredith had shed tears reading the account, and tears burned her eyes now as she prayed for the words to soothe the hurt she had caused with her thoughtlessness. Taking a deep breath, she lifted her head and went after Stark.

Chapter Five

Stark stood against the wall next to the trash can, his thumbs hooked in his belt, one knee bent, the sole of his booted foot braced against the cool sheet metal. The raised channels of the siding bit into his shoulder blades while storm-gray clouds scudded against a gunmetal sky. The weather suited his mood, but on that day four years ago it had been warm and bright and clear, a perfect day for driving, for giving thanks. A day of death.

A whiff of coconut danced on the warm, rain-scented air. Everything in him tightened, alerted, but then Meredith stepped through the stable door, and against his will, against common sense, against everything he knew and wanted, he relaxed. It was as if, now that she knew, he could no longer maintain his distance. She had breached the chasm with her knowledge of his dark past, his great loss. He wanted to hate her for that. Instead, he felt a pathetic relief.

Putting his head back against the cold metal siding, he drew air in through his nostrils and asked, "How did you find out?"

He cut his eyes down to find her bowing her head as if in shame. "I did an internet search last night after you left and read a newspaper account of the accident."

Stark sighed and shifted around. "The truck trailer turned over on my wife's car. I was driving. Catherine and Belinda were sitting on the passenger side, Cathy in the front, Bel in the back." He closed his eyes. "I was knocked out. Couple broken bones. Bel died instantly, Cathy on the way to the hospital."

"Four years ago today," Meredith whispered, tears spilling from her eyes. "I'm so sorry, Stark." She reached out a hand, but he stepped back, straightening. Something told him he'd break if she touched him just then, shatter into pieces too small ever to reassemble.

He cleared his throat of a sudden lump. "I didn't know until almost twenty-four hours later. So I'm never quite sure which date should be emblazoned in my memory."

"Both," Meredith said. "Every day, actually. Each and every day with them should be commemorated in some way."

Astounded by the idea, he shook his head, confessing, "Mostly I just try to forget."

"But that's impossible, isn't it? And why would you forget when that would mean letting go of all the good times?"

Good times that were over and gone. Good times that broke his heart.

Frowning, he shook his head. "Are you telling me that you don't try to forget the awful thing that happened to you?"

She folded her arms, her hands chaffing her sleeves as if she was suddenly chilled. "That's different."

"Is it?"

One of her hands crept up and rubbed a spot above her left breast. "Yes. I didn't know the man who attacked me, had no history with him. If it hadn't been me, it would have been some other woman. There's nothing pleasant or happy to remember about him, other than the fact that he didn't manage to kill me."

Anger roared through Stark. "He tried to kill you?"

She nodded, shivering. "He told me to be quiet and let him do what he wanted and he wouldn't hurt me, but I screamed and struggled," she said in a low, husky voice. "So he stabbed me."

Stark felt himself shaking and knotted his hands into fists to quell the motion. "He literally stabbed you?"

Once again she touched the spot on the left side of her chest. "My necklace deflected the blade. I have a scar, but the cut wasn't even nearly fatal, and he didn't get a second chance because people heard me and ran to my rescue."

"That must've been some necklace."

She dipped her fingers into her sweater and pulled out a chain with a gold cross dangling from it. It was about two inches long and maybe three-eighths-of-an-inch wide at its heart, and it showed a definite dent. "I always wear it."

"Wow. I can see why." He stepped closer, cupping the cross in his hand. A fraction of an inch either way and she wouldn't be here now. "Did they catch him?"

She shook her head. "No."

Frustration simmered in Stark. He dropped the necklace and stepped back. "How do you deal with that?"

Shrugging, she tucked the necklace back into her sweater. "Any way I can."

"When did this happen?" he asked, struggling to keep his anger leashed.

Head tilted, she seemed to have to actually think about it. "Over three years ago now. Yes, it was three years in June."

She'd been all of twenty-three at the time. "And you didn't come home after it happened?"

"I couldn't. I have to work." Looking up at the roiling clouds, she softly added, "Besides, I wasn't going to let him take anything more than I had to. He took my sense of power and safety, my trust in my fellow man, my natural tendency to give everyone the benefit of the doubt. For a while, he took my joy, my happiness. I'm still working on opening up." She looked down, adding, "I've never told my family."

Shocked, Stark felt his eyebrows jump, not because he didn't understand. This he understood only too well. Some pains were too personal, too deep and incapacitating to talk about. No, he was shocked because he truly hadn't expected to hold something so uniquely in common with her. He had a difficult time talking about his trauma even with those who knew of his loss.

"They won't hear about it from me," he promised. "No one will."

She looked him squarely in the eye then, and softly said, "I know."

Both shaken and warmed, he felt the sharp edge of a moist wind at his back. Without even realizing he was going to do it, he took hold of her, his hand completely encircling her arm just above the elbow. The contact rocked him. Apparently it jolted her, too, for she looked down, jerking slightly.

"We'd better go in," he said, feeling a tingly warmth flow through him, as if his nerve endings were awakening. "Rain's coming."

Casting another glance at the sky, she let him turn her through the door and back into the darkened interior of the stable. Horses shifted and blew, content in their stalls. Rex and one of the hands had been in earlier to turn them out and drop new feed. Most had wandered back in to eat. Stark had closed stall gates to ensure that none of the animals got curious and bothered Soldier. The pair of horses that had remained in the paddock came trotting in with the wind, seeking the comfort of their stalls. Stark pulled Meri back against the wall until the horses settled, then quickly closed the remaining open gates.

Soldier hadn't yet fully roused, but he swung his big head and blew through his nostrils, making guttural sounds as if testing his throat. Stark trickled some water deep into the animal's mouth in case his throat was dry, and the old stud settled somewhat. When he turned back to Meredith, he found her perched atop the feed barrel, watching him, a small smile playing about her pretty lips.

No woman had looked at him with any apparent appreciation since Cathy had died. It unnerved him. Just as he was about to suggest that she ought to get back to the house to see about Wes, the deluge hit, drumming against the metal roof over their heads like dull thunder.

He pushed a hand over his face and tried to think what to say, but she beat him to it, asking in a purely conversational tone, "How'd you wind up in Ponca City?"

The simple, true answer seemed the easiest. "I bought into a practice there. My partner was older, looking to retire and leave the practice in good hands." He could have left it at that, but for some reason he went on. "I married his daughter. It was a good life. When he retired, I took on another partner. Then, when Cathy died, I walked away from it all." He shook his head and gave her the unvarnished truth. "I ran." He parked his hands at his belt and admitted, "That's how I wound up here."

Meri said nothing to that, just pulled up one knee and hugged it. "I read that the truck driver apologized over and over before he died."

Cocking his own knee, Stark looked at the scuffed and scarred toe of his old boot. "That's what they told me." Again, he spilled his guts for no good reason. "That's always been one of the worst parts, not knowing who to be mad at—him or me."

"You?" she yelped. "Why would you be mad at yourself?"

So he told her how he'd delayed their departure that day so he could watch a football game on TV. "My dad's a coach. If I couldn't watch the game with him, I wanted to be able to at least discuss it with him. I mean, isn't that what Thanksgiving is *really* about?" he asked in disgust.

"Thanksgiving?" she echoed uncertainly. It was October, after all, not November.

"It was our year to spend the actual holiday with Cathy's folks," he explained, leaning against the stall wall, "so we were on our way to celebrate with my family a month early. The Burns family has a tradition, a month of Thanksgiving. That way they can work in all the in-laws and grandparents."

"Sounds like a good plan."

"Yeah, until somebody gets killed."

For a moment she said nothing to that. Then very softly she ventured, "It's impossible to make sense of that."

"No kidding."

"I'm not sure everything is supposed to make sense to us now," she said carefully. "I think that some things simply must be accepted. Sometimes, I think that's all God expects of us, just our acceptance."

Part of him rebelled at the very idea. Just accept as his lot in life, the senseless deaths of his wife and daughter? He'd never be able to do that! Yet, another part of him, a part he didn't even want to acknowledge but couldn't quite deny, reached hungrily for that acceptance, as if along that way lay peace. But did it? How could it possibly?

Abruptly, as if God had shut off a faucet, the rain stopped. Soldier bobbed his head and swished his tail, blowing gently through his nostrils as he nosed Stark's pocket for possible food. In that instant, Stark made a decision. Rather, he acknowledged the decision that he'd already made.

"You have a job with me as soon as your dad and this old horse can spare you."

Meri hopped off the barrel, beaming. "Oh, Stark! Thank you!"

For all the world, she looked as if she might hug him. He got out of there before she could do or say anything to change his mind, snagging his kit on the way and calling out that he would be back.

What, he wondered, had he gotten himself into? One thing was certain—his quiet, solitary existence had just come to an end. He could only hope he wouldn't live to regret it.

She didn't see him for two days. Meri wasn't sure why she'd avoided Stark. She sat on the porch swing, swaddled in one of her dad's old sweaters, holding a cup of hot tea while trying to puzzle it out. She had misjudged him, chalking up his curmudgeonly ways to personality and nothing more. Once she knew the tragic truth, she found herself unsure of a lot of things. She even began to wonder why she'd never told her family about the attack.

Oh, she'd told herself that she hadn't wanted to worry them, that they were still processing her mom's sudden death, that they'd insist she give up nursing and come home like a child who needed supervision. The old reasons seemed shallow and silly now, and as long as she could come up with no satisfactory answers, she felt compelled to keep her distance, especially from Stark. And she couldn't say why.

He'd always bothered her. Something about him had always dug at her, like an itch beneath her skin, something she couldn't quite scratch. When he'd touched her to guide her into shelter, she'd been stunned. He'd done exactly what her attacker had done before he'd dragged her between the cars and turned her to face him. He'd taken her by the arm, just above the elbow. Her attacker had done it to keep her from running. Stark had meant only to steer her to safety out of the storm, and even as she'd been prepared to recoil, she hadn't. Instead, all she'd felt was... She didn't know what she'd felt. Lightning?

Thinking about it now, she couldn't help asking herself if working with Stark would be the smart thing to do. After all, she was a trained registered nurse. What did she know about veterinary medicine? What did she really know about him? When it came right down to it, she'd guessed that she'd blown any chance of working for him, but then he'd surprised her with the job offer. Without a single detail, she'd leaped at it and then wondered afterward what she'd gotten herself into.

How like her. She'd done the same thing with nursing. At the time, so soon after her mom's unexpected death, nursing had seemed like the right thing. Only later had she realized that the odds of being able to work close to home were slim to none, which left her with exactly two options. It was Stark or return to Oklahoma City.

As if in answer to that dilemma, Stark Burns appeared on the pathway, his dark hat and denim jacket dappled with morning light through the rusty leaves overhead. His truck had been parked on the side of the road all night again, but he hadn't come to the house either of the last two mornings. Meredith had left Stark's coffee and breakfast for Rex to take when he went to turn out the horses. Rex had returned both mornings behaving as if nothing was out of the ordinary, relaying brief instructions for her concerning Soldier's care during the day while Stark had to be away seeing to other patients. Stark himself had not put in an appearance until now. He stopped at the edge of the porch and lifted one booted foot, propping it against the edge of the porch floor.

After pushing back his hat, he crossed his hands over his knee and leaned forward. "Horse is much improved."

Meredith let out a breath of relief. "Glad to hear it. I thought so myself yesterday."

"He's standing on his own and eating his mash, but I'm going to leave the IV and sling in place through today, just to make sure he's getting plenty of nutrition and fluids. We'll untether him this evening. You'll need to check on him a couple times during the night."

"No problem."

"I'll check him daily for a while. Then we can leave him be."

"Sounds good. Will you tell Dad? He'll want to hear it from you."

"I'm not exactly presentable," Stark said, stroking his unshaved jaw with his thumb and fingers. The gesture did strange things to Meri's breathing.

Setting aside her tea, she hopped up from the swing and shoved back the sleeves of the sweater, which hung to her knees. She chirped brightly, "Like Dad'll care."

Stark shifted his foot back to the ground and straightened, resettling his hat forward on his head. Meri gulped. Had he always been that good-looking? Turning abruptly, she hurried into the house, Stark following. She glanced back to see him removing his hat, but he kept it in hand. He paused when they passed through the kitchen and raised his hat in greeting to Callie, who sat at the table with Bodie.

"Morning, Stark," she said.

Unwilling to be left out, Bodie exclaimed, "Mor'in!" She then smiled, showing him her new teeth—and her breakfast.

"Morning, ladies," Stark said. "Callie, I want to thank you for having fed me so well during this time."

"Wasn't any bother," Callie said. "Are you done, then?"

"I think so."

"Well, that's good news, isn't it?"

"Yes, ma'am. I believe it is."

"Praise God!" Callie said, clasping her hands together. Bodie instantly bowed her head, obviously expecting to pray.

Meri smiled, holding back a chuckle. "We're just going to tell Dad," she explained.

She led Stark into the back hallway and tapped on her father's door.

"Come in," he called.

Meri walked into the room and found him sitting fully dressed on the hospital bed, his Bible open on his lap. "Daddy," she said, stepping aside, "Stark's got something to tell you."

Stark angled past her into her room, going to

lean a hip against the dresser. "Wes," he said, nodding in greeting, "you're looking better."

It was true. Her father had a healthy skin tone again, and his hair was beginning to grow back. It was just fuzz atop his head right now—and white fuzz at that—but hair, nonetheless. He seemed to have more energy lately, too.

"Never mind about me," Wes said, glancing hopefully between them. "How's my horse?"

"He's looking better, too," Stark said. He explained in detail, finishing with, "Barring any relapses, I think he'll recover fully."

Wes sighed richly, closed his eyes for a moment, then said, "That's music to these old ears. Thank you, Stark. We owe you a big one for this. Whatever it is, you just send the bill, and we'll gladly pay it."

Stark chuckled. "Wish all my clients were so willing. Of course, you will be getting the employee discount." He addressed Meri then. "That is not to say you'll be getting your first paycheck out of this. We'll consider tomorrow your first official day on the job."

Wes sat bolt upright on the bed. "Meri? Am I getting this right? You're going to work for Stark?"

Well, she could've handled this better. Smiling gamely, she stepped into the room and nodded. "That's right, Daddy. It's okay with you, isn't it, if I come home to stay?"

Before she knew what was happening, he was off the bed and coming around it, his arms opened wide. "Oh, sugar! This is wonderful news!"

Only then did she realize that some part of her had feared he *wouldn't* be thrilled, that he'd question her choices and decisions, had always secretly questioned them. Feeling her father's arms engulf her settled something for Meredith, healed something broken within her. She laughed, mostly to hide the tears that suddenly threatened her.

"She'll be a lot of help," she heard him tell Stark. "You wait and see. She's got the healing touch, my girl."

When she looked at Stark, his face seemed frighteningly blank. "So long as she's at the office on time in the mornings, I'll be happy," he said, straightening. "And speaking of time, I'd best be on my way."

Wes insisted on shaking hands with him. "Can't thank you enough. What a blessing you've been to this family."

"Just doing my job," Stark muttered. He sent a sharp look at Meri. "Want to walk me out? Got a few instructions for you."

"Sure."

Stark nodded a farewell to Wes and left the room. His long legs carried him swiftly through the house. Callie had apparently taken Bodie upstairs, which was just as well, considering the pace that Stark set. Meredith had to trot to keep up with him. As soon as they reached the front porch, he rounded on her.

"You didn't even tell them that you're going to work for me? I'm the poster boy for personal privacy, but even I would have shared that! What were you planning to do? Disappear for hours at a time and come up with a new story every day?"

"No! I just wanted to be sure it was going to work out before I said anything."

"You just wanted to be sure I wouldn't change my mind? Or you wanted to be sure that you liked the job first?"

"Neither!" she shot back.

He shoved a hand through his hair and carefully settled his hat into place. "Every time I begin to think I've got you figured out," he muttered, "you throw me a curve."

"I don't mean to."

Stepping close, he lowered his voice and asked, "Why didn't you tell your folks about what happened to you? You were...attacked. Stabbed. You could've *died*."

She looked away, the old answers rolling off her tongue. "My family was still trying to deal with my mother's passing. It wouldn't have changed anything. Why worry them when they could do nothing? Rex's first marriage was a mess, and Dad was grieving. Ann's high-pressure job—" She stopped, unable to go on and oddly shamed.

What was it about Stark Burns that made her unable to lie to him? She'd told these lies to herself over and over again, but she couldn't tell them to him.

"Meri?" he asked softly.

Gulping down a rapidly growing lump in her throat, she ducked her head and said, "Telling them would have made it too real."

He was silent for several seconds. Then he shifted his weight from one foot to the other and said softly, "I understand. They'd have wanted to discuss it, investigate it, do something about it."

She nodded. "Find a way to protect me. I couldn't let it be that real."

He sighed deeply. "I get it."

"It's more than that," she admitted quickly, finally looking up at him. "How well do you know my sister?"

Shrugging, he shook his head. "I know she used to manage some hotel in Dallas."

"Some hotel?" Meri scoffed. "Just one of the largest luxury hotels in the country."

"Okay. So?"

Meredith flapped a hand helplessly. "I've never measured up to Ann. She could always hold her own with Rex and Dad. She was always out in the field with them, while I was here at the house with Mom, learning to cook and clean, all the girly things. Ann was a big athletic star at War Bonnet High." Meri folded her arms, pushing up the sleeves of Wes's sweater. "They don't give medals for outstanding home economics students."

Stark chuckled. "So what? Cathy was an outstanding home ec student. She made a great home." He sounded so wistful that Meredith wanted to put her arms around him. Instead, she walked to the swing where he'd found her and plopped down again.

"Ann would've handled it differently," she said morosely. "She'd have taken that attacker's knife and stabbed *him*."

"That's rubbish," Stark stated matter-of-factly. "You're just beating up on yourself to keep from telling me why you didn't want your family to know you're going to work for me."

"Wrong," she said primly. "I was just waiting to confirm God's will on the matter."

In a blink he went from understanding to blazingly angry. Once again, Meredith's heart dropped and her prayers winged Heavenward.

Oh, Lord, what have I done now? *And how do I undo it?*

Chapter Six

"What's God got to do with it?" Stark demanded.

He'd have shaken her if he'd dared to put his hands on her. She could talk to him about God after all she'd been through, knowing all she knew about him?

"But, Stark," she said, blinking at him, "don't you believe we should seek God's will in our lives?"

"You think God cares what happens to us?"

"Absolutely."

"Was it God's will for you to be attacked at knifepoint?"

"No," she answered firmly. "We live in a fallen world, Stark. People act against God's will all the time. He doesn't want it that way, but it's their choice."

That seemed mighty convenient to him.

"Who acted against God's will the day my family died?" he demanded. "Did I act against God's will when I watched that football game before my family and I left to visit my parents?"

"Don't be silly."

"Was the truck driver acting against God's will when he took that ramp too fast?"

"People make mistakes, Stark."

"Maybe I should've had Cathy drive, put my daughter on the other side of the car, sped up, slowed down! What would have made God happy, do you think?"

"Stop it, Stark," Meredith said quietly.

"Just don't tell me that it was God's will my family died," he growled at her, stepping off the porch.

"I'd never do that," she said, rising from the swing and following him as far as the edge of the porch.

Part of him wished she'd come after him, but then what? He closed his mind to the very thought of it. If he had a lick of sense, he'd tell her to forget working for him. Instead, he barked over his shoulder, "Eight a.m., and if you're late, don't even bother coming."

She said nothing to that, not that he waited around to hear it.

Reaching the ditch on the edge of that red-dirt road, he stepped over it in one long stride. Two more brought him to the door of his truck. He yanked it open hard enough to feel it buck in his hand. Angry now just for being so angry, he swept off his hat and spun it into the cab before folding himself down behind the steering wheel. There he finally paused long enough to catch his breath and drop his head into his hands.

He hadn't been this angry since Cathy and Bel had died. He didn't know what that meant, but somehow he had to find his equilibrium again. Maybe spending the night in his own bed for a change would give him back his perspective, help him find that calm numbness that allowed him to cope with life as it existed now. That and work were the only answers he had at the moment, the only answers he'd ever had.

Starting up the truck, he whipped a U-turn and headed out to keep the day's appointments. He hadn't reached the first section line when his phone started ringing, and so it went, all day long, one call after another. He could barely manage the day's appointments for fielding or returning calls.

By the time he returned to the Straight Arrow to check on Soldier, he hadn't managed to change or shower, let alone shave.

He'd missed lunch. Again. Stark removed Soldier's IV bag and shunt, disappointed that Meri didn't show up to help with the latter. At least Rex arrived to assist with the block and tackle supporting the sling.

"Dad's in the shower," Rex explained, holding Soldier's head while Stark unbuckled the sling. "Meri won't leave the house until he's settled again."

Stark nodded. "No problem. She knows what to do from here on out."

"Could've knocked me over with a feather when I heard she's gonna work for you," Rex went on.

Trying not to react, Stark asked, "Who told you?"

"Dad," Rex answered, stroking the horse's neck and leading him forward to walk him out of the sling that now lay on the ground. "He was gushing about it."

Wes, then. Not Meredith.

"Mmm-hmm." Bending to fold up the sling, Stark kept his face averted. He had to wonder just how likely it was that Meredith would still show up in the morning.

Rex closed the stall gate behind Soldier and went for the ladder tucked into the far corner of the stable. The two men quickly set up the ladder. Stark climbed up and retrieved his block and tackle, leaving the hook in the beam in case it was needed later. When he came down, Rex clapped him on the shoulder.

"This is going to be good for Meri," he said. "She changed after she moved to the City. I can't quite put my finger on it, but..." He shrugged. "I don't know. Maybe she's just not cut out for nursing."

"If she's too softhearted for nursing, she's too softhearted for working with animals," Stark warned.

"No, it's not that." Rex shook his head. "Oh, she's softhearted, all right. Meri's always been sweet as pie."

"Is that right?" Stark muttered. Couldn't prove it by how she was with him.

"But she's got her own kind of strength. You know? Mom was that way. Grandma always said Mom smoothed the rough edges off Dad. I didn't get that until I met Callie. You know what I mean?"

In a strange way, Stark did. He'd felt like nothing but rough, ragged edges since Cathy had died. He supposed he'd be that way the rest of his life, sharp, broken, jagged edges. He almost hated Rex in that moment.

"Gotta get moving," he rumbled. "Want my dinner and a solid bed."

"You're welcome to eat with us," Rex offered, but Stark declined.

"Naw, I'm not fit company. Haven't showered in two days. Thanks all the same." Bundling up his gear, he started for the door. "I'll be by tomorrow."

"Sleep well, man. And, Stark?"

He paused without looking back. "Yep?"

"This thing with Meri, it'll work good for you, too. I know it will."

Nodding, Stark went on his way. He wasn't convinced she'd show up or that her doing so would be a good thing for either of them, but time, he supposed, would tell. And what, after all, did he really have except time? Too much empty, hollow time.

When he returned from the diner at seven forty-five the next morning, Meredith was waiting in the small, dusty parking area in front of his building. He'd converted an old house about a block west of the Feed & Grain on the edge of War Bonnet. The porch had been falling off the front of the small clapboard structure, so he'd simply razed it and installed a pair of broad, concrete steps. Then he'd turned the garage out back into a kennel and connected the two buildings with a modern operating suite and passageway. A metal carport doubled as a temporary stable when necessary.

The former vet in this area, now deceased, had lived miles out of town on a ranch of his own and hadn't bothered with small animals. Stark liked the small-animal part of his practice as much as the large-animal part, so he tried to be available to every patient that needed him. It wasn't easy. He didn't see how having Meredith on staff could improve that situation, but if he had a goal in hiring her, the small-animal part was it.

Somewhat surprised—and more relieved than he wanted to admit even to himself—to see her there, he stopped his truck beside her small car and rolled down the window, waiting until she did the same. "Follow me around back. I'll show you where to park."

She drove her car around the building behind him. He intended to point her to the spot next to the carport and keep his regular space for himself, but he didn't like the idea of her trudging outside in inclement weather, so at the last moment he took the spot beside the carport and waved her in under the shelter. She looked surprised when she got out of the car, wearing pale blue scrubs and athletic shoes, her long strawberry blond hair in a ponytail.

"I sometimes use this space as a stable for large animals," he warned her, and decided in that instant to have another carport installed. Why not? He could afford it, and he'd have use for it even after she was gone. For she would surely go, probably sooner rather than later. He had no illusions about how easy he was to get along with these days and no wish or intention to change.

Keeping such thoughts to himself, he took out his keys and unlocked the back entry, nodding at the outdoor shower tucked into one corner of the carport. The area could be closed off with a curtain attached to a circular rod. "I sometimes come in filthy. I've had to shower in my clothes more times than I can count just to enter the building."

"Must be cold in the winter," she commented.

He shrugged. "It's okay if the water's hot enough."

"Well, at least you don't have any neighbors."

"Just the Feed & Grain. All the land between me and them is theirs, and what's on the other side is mine."

"So you've got some acreage here," she said as they stepped up into the narrow back hall.

"About ten acres of red dirt and weeds. Someone sometime thought they'd build some houses out here, so they leveled all the trees. Guess it didn't pan out."

"Ever thought of throwing up a fence and sowing some grass, maybe keeping a horse?"

"Don't know when I'd have time to actually ride."

"Well, just sow the grass then, keep the dust from blowing."

"And have to mow," he pointed out, leading the way past floor-to-ceiling storage cabinets. "Two treatment rooms on the left. One's pretty dusty." He turned right. "Reception area."

"You don't have a computer."

"Laptop's in the truck. I'll get another in here for you."

"There's no phone."

"Everything comes to my cell."

She gave him an exasperated look. "So you answer all your own calls...while you're treating patients. How's *that* working for you?"

He made a face. "Bane of my existence, but how else was I going to handle it?"

"You should've hired someone from the get-go, Doctor."

"Yeah, yeah. I'll get a phone installed."

"Until then, have the calls rerouted to my phone," she suggested, pulling out her cell phone.

He made another face. "I suppose that'll do until I can get an office phone in here. I guess you'll need my personal number, too."

"That would help," she said, "and you'll need mine." They worked for some minutes to get everything set up correctly. Once that was done, she said, "Oh, we have to synchronize our calendars."

He frowned. "This is getting more complicated by the second."

"But it will be simpler in the long run," she promised. "I'll answer your business calls, make appointments, send you notifications and relay any emergency messages. You'll be free to work and answer the phone only when it's necessary. I'll also be here to help out with any patients that come through the door and can go into the field with you whenever you need extra hands."

He wasn't convinced, but then the phone rang. Her phone. She glanced at the screen, tapped an icon and held the phone to her ear. "War Bonnet Veterinary Services. How may I help you?" She listened, then said, "I'm Dr. Burns's assistant, Meredith. Just let me check his calendar. One moment please." She quickly checked the calendar and got back on the phone. "The doctor is going to be in your area around four this afternoon. I'll ask him to stop by when he's completed that call and will get back to you with an approximate arrival time. Will that do?" Looking at Stark, she raised her eyebrows.

"Probably around five-fifteen," he whispered.

"Most likely around five-fifteen," she said, "but I'll let you know when he leaves the other location. Yes. Thank you."

When she hung up, she sent the notification so he'd have a record of the address and problem.

"There. Now, what else do you need? You have to be ordering your own supplies and doing all your own sterilization. The sterilization I can do now. The other I'll learn quickly." She glanced around the tiny waiting area and said, "First, though, I've got to do some cleaning up around here. Really, when was the last time you dusted?"

He grinned, feeling suddenly lighter. Maybe this was going to work out, after all. "I've never dusted."

"Well, there you are."

"You can dust after I leave," he said, checking his wristwatch. "Right now I need to show you the kennel. We have a spayed Chihuahua that needs looking after until her owner arrives."

"A Chihuahua? Really?"

"Yep. She should be waking up shortly."

The office cat slunk out from under the built-in desk and twined itself through Meredith's ankles. Stark bent to scoop him up, rising again to introduce him. "This is Clunker."

"I didn't know you had a cat."

He shrugged. "We need a mouser around here. He's not declawed and comes and goes at will through a pet door in the foyer. Otherwise, you could bring your cat up here." She scratched the gray mouser's ears and was rewarded with a loud, uneven purr.

"I've never heard a cat make that sound."

"That's why he's called Clunker. Can't find any reason for it, though I'm sure there is one."

He put down the cat, and it streaked off. Stark led Meredith back to the kennel. The pup was awake and began yipping piteously as soon as it saw them. Noticing a soft animal bed on the floor, Meredith proposed lining it with a sterile pad and taking the puppy up front with her. Stark saw no harm in it. He showed her where to find the preprinted care-instruction sheet for the owner and then told her that she could call the owner to pick up the puppy any time after eleven o'clock that morning. He usually took care of those things on his lunch hour, late evening or early morning.

"You can knock off at five," he told her, "whether I'm back or not. Just be sure to have my calls rerouted to my phone again. Oh, and don't forget to lock up. I'll see about getting you a key of your own, but for now just turn the dead bolt on the front door and press the lock on the doorknob when you go out the back."

"All right. Let me know if you need me to do anything special today."

"Will do."

Strangely, he felt as if he ought not to just walk out. He'd always at least kissed his wife on the cheek before he'd left for the day, but he couldn't do that with Meri, of course. In the end, he patted her lightly on the shoulder as he walked past her.

He felt somewhat encouraged and wildly off balance at the same time. Something told him that wasn't going to change anytime soon.

By 2:00 p.m. on Saturday, quitting time, Meredith had the entire clinic, including the kennel, gleaming. She'd organized the reception desk and decorated the waiting area as pleasingly as she could manage with what she had on hand—a couple of vases she'd found tucked into a cupboard and some framed landscape photographs that she'd liberated from the attic at the Straight Arrow. She had no idea who'd taken the pictures, but she recognized some of the shots as being Straight Arrow property. Stark seemed not to notice.

Because he often worked late, he apparently sometimes napped at the office and perhaps even stayed over on occasion, as there was a bed in one of the rooms, as well as a dresser. The bed had no headboard or footboard and only a single, pilled blanket for cover. The dresser was chipped in several places. She hadn't peeked in the drawers or the closet, but she assumed that he kept clean clothing there, and she'd found toiletries in the single restroom.

He hadn't bothered having the old cast-iron bathtub removed from that room. The thing couldn't be more than a foot deep and was a horrible shade of pink, but the other fixtures were new and gleaming white. Without asking, she'd hung a plain white curtain in front of the tub, and he hadn't said a word about it. She thought it gave the room a more businesslike feel.

She had even gone out and scrubbed the freestanding shower in the corner of the carport. Then she'd replaced the curtain there with a heavier, two-layer one and laid a clean mat on the ground outside of it so he wouldn't have to step onto the cold brick with bare feet. He hadn't mentioned those changes, either, but so long as he didn't complain, she assumed that he approved.

Wandering around the empty place on Saturday, she took stock, wondering what she could do to dress up the place next. Her eye fell on the longest wall of the waiting area. Stark had painted the whole place a clean, utilitarian beige. Then he'd fitted every available space with black wall cabinets and other fixtures as needed, everywhere except in the sleeping room. He'd had the hardwood floors refinished throughout the house, too.

She thought she might warm up the place with a darker shade of paint on the larger wall in the waiting area, and perhaps she could find a lamp to brighten up things. Next week promised to be busier because now that he had office help, people were making appointments for their small pets. Plus, her new computer would be delivered from Ardmore on

Tuesday, so she could start keeping up with patient files for him. Still...

Why not come in early on Monday morning and get the job done before he even showed up? It wouldn't take long to paint that one wall, and he would be surprised. Besides, if the pattern held true, he wouldn't complain—or likely even comment—once the change was made. Two or three hours should be plenty of time.

She made her plans and gathered her supplies that afternoon, driving into Ardmore to purchase everything. Her dad felt well enough to ride along, though he stayed in the car while she went into the store to pick out paint. She chose a shade called Burnt Leather. While the clerk was mixing it, she picked up a kit that included all she needed to complete the job. Everything else she'd used at the veterinary clinic she'd brought from the ranch, but this she paid for herself. It would be her gift to Stark, a way to thank him for taking a chance on her.

Rising before daylight on Monday, she dressed in her usual scrubs, then donned one of her dad's oldest shirts for protection from splatters and tied a bandanna around her head before hurrying over to the veterinary clinic. She parked in front because it would be easier and quicker to haul in her supplies that way. There would be plenty of time to move the car around to the back before Stark came in that morning.

She turned on the light in the waiting area and began moving the two side tables to the end of the counter that separated the receptionist's desk from the waiting area. She set the vases atop the counter. Then she started moving the chairs lined up against the wall, stacking them in the far corner. She was lifting the third chair when Stark's angry voice startled her.

"What do you think you're doing?"

She jumped back, catching the edge of the plastic roller pan with her foot. Thankfully, it was still empty of paint, but it flipped, sending brushes, masking tape and a stir stick flying. She clapped a hand to her chest, trying to calm her suddenly galloping heart.

"You scared me."

"You scared me! I thought some thief was after drugs."

"No. I was just going to paint. Spruce up the place a bit."

He shoved a hand through hair already on end. That was when she realized he was standing there in bare feet, his jeans hastily pulled on, his T-shirt inside out. He obviously hadn't shaved.

"Do you have to change everything, Meredith?" he demanded. "And does it have to be done right away?"

"I—I'm just trying to help," she said lamely. "I didn't realize you had a late call last night and would be sleeping over."

The dark slashes of his brows drew together. "Sleeping over? What do you mean sleeping over? I always sleep here."

She goggled at that. "Always?"

Throwing his hands wide impatiently, he demanded, "Where else would I sleep?"

Blinking at him, she ventured, "At home?"

He looked at her like she'd suddenly sprouted a third eye in the center of her forehead. "This *is* my home."

Dumbfounded, she couldn't speak or even seem to think for several seconds. Then suddenly everything toppled in on her at once.

"But you don't even have a kitchen here! Or a television o-or...anything."

"I don't need that stuff," he muttered, folding his arms.

"But how do you eat?"

"There's a perfectly good diner right up the street," he said, jerking his chin.

She lifted her eyebrows at that. "Really? You eat there three times a day?"

He made a scoffing sound. "I can't remember the last time I ate three times in a day."

"Then why—"

"It's all I need," he interrupted, dropping his arms.

"All you need?" she asked softly. "Or all you'll allow yourself?"

"Now you're just prying," he retorted coolly, "not to mention keeping me from getting much-needed sleep! Will you get out of here? Your working hours are eight to five."

She saw it all clearly then, the lengths to which he went to punish himself. The question was, how far would he go to punish her if she actually did improve things around here? Well, let him do his worst—stubborn, foolish, silly man. She wasn't going to stand by and let him wallow in undeserved guilt.

Inclining her head, she calmly said, "Yes, sir."

She bent to pick up a brush, but he barked, "Leave it!"

Snatching back her hand, she swept out the door and into her car. So much for her gesture of gratitude. She supposed she should be thankful he hadn't fired her on the spot.

She didn't realize she was crying until she

felt the first tear drip off her chin and plop onto her chest. Then she had to decide why she was crying.

Because Stark had yelled at her?

No. She'd had irascible doctors yell at her plenty of times. It came with the job.

Because he wasn't as appreciative of her efforts as she'd hoped?

No. She'd known he might be hiding his irritation, and she couldn't be anything but pleased by his thoughtfulness and patience.

She cried because he seemed intent on punishing himself for the deaths of his family. Stark's life consisted of work and nothing more. He didn't even allow himself the barest of creature comforts. The man showered outside, for pity's sake! She hated to think of him eating all of his meals at the diner. Their food was bland at best. That had to have gotten old very fast. Yet, what were his options? There was a microwave on the premises for warming things, but he couldn't cook much in that, and she hadn't seen any dishes or kitchenware of any kind in the place. No wonder he was so slender.

What a sad, lonely, uncomfortable way to live.

All this time she'd been trying to fix up

the clinic when what was really needed was a cure for the doctor.

All right, Lord, she prayed silently, *I get it now, so show me the cure and how to give it to him. It won't be easy, but You can do it. I'll help. Whatever You want me to do, I'll do it. For him and for You.*

Chapter Seven

She came back with breakfast. Astounded after the way he'd practically tossed her out on her ear earlier, Stark grumbled, but he didn't have the heart to turn away her offering, especially as the oatmeal still steamed, teeming with plump cranberries and crisp walnuts. She'd brought butter, cinnamon and brown sugar to top it off, along with a thermos of black coffee and a container of juice. He wouldn't find anything to touch such a breakfast at the diner and ate the whole enormous bowlful in mere minutes. Afterward, he had to stop himself from licking the bowl. That Callie could sure cook.

By way of apology for growling at her earlier, he finished moving the furniture in the waiting area out of the way so she could paint, though he shuddered to think what color might wind up on his wall. He returned late that evening, pleasantly surprised to find the waiting area wall a rich brown. The framed photos she'd hung looked especially good now, and he wondered where she'd gotten the black wrought-iron lamp with the leather shade.

He went into his bedroom and found an old quilt, soft with age, draped across the foot of his bed, a rag rug on the floor. The Straight Arrow must be practically denuded by now, though he didn't remember seeing any of the things around here in the ranch house. He shook his head against the smile tugging at the corners of his lips and went to gather clean clothes so he could shower.

She showed up early with breakfast every other morning that week. He stopped even planning to go to the diner for that meal, but her generosity came with a price. How could he not tell her that he liked the paint color she'd chosen and the other changes she'd made around the place? So, of course, she made a few *more* changes.

His shabby bedroom curtains disappeared and new ones took their place. Then she painted a wall in his room the same color as the wall in the waiting area, and the next thing he knew silk sunflowers were poking up out of the vases in the waiting area and a long, embroidered cloth graced the top of his dresser. The place started to smell like cinnamon instead of antiseptic.

He was still busy, but life had calmed somewhat, and he found himself getting home earlier. Stranger still, he was happier to get there. He had time to read some of the journals and articles that he'd neglected and needed to keep up with.

The computer had arrived. The phone had been hooked up, and he'd realized that it would be a good idea to have internet service. That's when Meri had pointed out that he could download TV programs and movies to watch on his computer. Suddenly, relaxation seemed a definite possibility.

"You could get another refrigerator, too," she said. He had one strictly for medications and samples that needed cooling. "Put it in your room, keep milk, cheese, fruit and lunch meat. You wouldn't have to eat out every meal."

"I don't eat out every meal now," he pointed out, cutting a look at her from the corner of his eye.

"You could eat out less."

"I'll think about it."

He was seeing a sick calf halfway to Ardmore that afternoon and decided he could use her help with it. She seemed pleased that he took her along and was as much help as he'd expected, which meant that he finished quickly, so he drove on to the appliance store. The smile she gave him was worth the price of the small refrigerator she picked out. She babbled so happily about what an asset the refrigerator would be that the clerk naturally assumed they were a couple setting up housekeeping.

"We're not married," Meredith said, but then color bloomed in her cheeks as she realized the implications of that. "I mean, he isn't…"

Stark cleared his throat, coming to her rescue. "Nurse Billings. Would you wait in the truck while I take care of this?"

"Yes, Doctor. Thank you."

He used his remote to open the cab for her, paid for the refrigerator with a company credit card and walked out to join her. She sat staring through the passenger window. Taking his time starting up the engine, he waited, but she didn't even acknowledge his presence until he quipped, "That's not my foot in your mouth."

She glared at him. And then she laughed. Laughing along with her felt good.

The next morning she brought in a plate of

scrambled eggs, bacon and toast, along with a bag of groceries to stock the fridge.

"Can you stay a little late today?" he asked, taking the extra chair she'd placed at the receptionist's desk for him.

"Sure."

Nodding, he tucked into the food. "They're installing another carport this afternoon, and they might not be finished by the time you leave. I need you to sign off on the job."

"No problem."

"I'll be out at the ranch this morning checking on Soldier. I can let them know you might be late, if you want."

"That'll work."

"Two surgeries scheduled Monday," he reminded her.

"I haven't forgotten."

"And, um, I might need your help tomorrow. With a pair of goats."

"Goats. So in the field."

"Better wear jeans and boots. And maybe bring a change of clothes. These particular goats don't react well to bright colors. Or men."

"Okay."

He finished his breakfast, got up and gathered his jacket and hat. They were going into the middle of November, and the weather had turned nippy.

"How much do I owe you for the groceries?" he asked lightly.

She shook her head. "That's all right." Her hand sneaked up to pat the pocket in the top of her gaily printed scrubs.

"Look, borrowing stuff from the ranch house is one thing. I can even handle you carrying in breakfast, but I draw the line at groceries. Where's the receipt?" he asked firmly. She looked down at her toes. "Am I going to have to search your pockets?" Suddenly, he very much wanted to search her pockets. Rocked by the impulse, he stepped back.

Her gaze moving up, she pulled the folded slip of paper from her pocket. Careful not to let their fingers touch, he took it from her, noted the amount and passed it back to her.

He walked out then, muttering, "Call if you need me."

What had possessed him to threaten to search her? After what she'd been through, that was the last thing he should do. After what he'd been through, it was the last thing he should *want* to do. He wouldn't be surprised if she quit that afternoon.

But she wouldn't.

Wrinkling his forehead in confusion, he

snugged on his hat and threw on his jacket before going out to his truck. He didn't know how he knew, but Meredith wouldn't quit on him. Even if he'd quit on himself, she wouldn't. He didn't know how he felt about that. He didn't *want* to know how he felt about that.

Thankfully, the day got busy in a hurry. Before he even got to his first appointment, Meri called to say that a fence had broken and a cow had been hit by a car. She'd already let his regularly scheduled appointment know he'd be late. Sadly, he couldn't do anything but put down the animal. The day fell into a fast-paced rhythm, but he was only about a quarter-hour off schedule when he reached the Straight Arrow.

Going to the stable first, he checked out Soldier and found him recovering nicely. He went to the house to suggest to Wes that the horse be turned out for exercise. Wes, too, looked better than the last time Stark had seen him.

"I'm about ready to be turned loose myself," he announced happily. "Dr. Shorter says I can attend church on Sunday."

"That's good news."

"By Thanksgiving we'll get our first inkling whether this cure has taken. Meri says the chances are good."

"I'd think she would be the authority on it," Stark said.

"Absolutely. She's read up on it. She's reading up on animal medicine now, you know."

Stark hadn't known, but it made sense. "She's made lots of…improvements around the clinic." He'd almost said *changes*, but *improvements* was the truth.

"She makes improvements everywhere she goes," Wes declared, smiling.

Stark soon took his leave. As he was going through the kitchen, he stopped to speak to Callie.

"I want to thank you for sending breakfast with Meri every day. You really don't have to do that."

Callie wiped her hands on a dish towel. "I'm sorry?"

"Breakfast," he repeated. "I want you to know how much I appreciate what Meri brings in every morning."

"Well, you'd better tell her, then," Callie said, tossing away the towel. "I haven't been cooking your breakfast. Haven't been cooking hers, come to that."

He stared at her for several seconds, watching a smile spread across her face. So Meredith had been cooking his breakfast every morning. He nodded and left.

Why had Meri let him think that Callie was cooking for him? She must have known that he'd make that assumption. Did her cooking for him make Meri as uncomfortable as it did him? Did it please her as much? The whole issue felt like terribly dangerous ground all of a sudden.

Back in his truck, he headed down that red dirt road to his next appointment, but he couldn't help thinking of Meredith. Even after all she'd been through, Meredith's heart was soft toward others. She was a generous, caring, supportive woman. He couldn't believe she compared herself to her sister and found herself wanting. Ann was all right, but she didn't strike Stark as being nearly as compassionate and empathetic as Meri.

If he could find the man who'd hurt Meredith...

In an effort to push aside the anger welling up in him, Stark thought of Wes, fighting cancer, his family rallying around him. The whole Billings family were good people. Stark hoped that the cancer had been eradicated. He sometimes had to deal with it in animals, and it was always scary and expensive to treat. Most people didn't even try. He hated to think how Meri would react if the cancer took her dad. Would she blame herself?

"Lord, don't let it happen," he said. "Those folks believe. They count on You. Show them mercy. Please."

He realized with a shock what he was doing. Nine days. Meri Billings had worked for him nine days, and he was praying again. Without even thinking about it!

He hadn't prayed, really prayed, since his wife and daughter had died. He hadn't even thought he could.

What was happening? What was Meredith doing to him?

If he had an ounce of sense, any thought of self-preservation, he'd cut her loose now. Today.

But he wasn't going to do that. Not today. Not tomorrow.

Maybe he should be praying for himself, for his sanity, because letting this go on was surely asking for heartbreak. And he just could not endure any more of that.

"How did you survive this without me?" Meri chortled as Stark braced his hands against the top rung of the low fence and hopped over it to safety, a pair of dark hooves lashing out yet again in his direction.

"I told you," he said with undisguised disgust, "they hate men."

"I believe you," Meri said, trying not to grin.

Crouched between the two goats, which were snugged to the wall of the barn by halters, she had performed as much of an examination as possible, following Stark's precise instructions. Every time he even leaned in too close, however, one of the goats tried to kick or bite him. Just getting the goats rounded up and into the barn had been a carnival act, and Meri was convinced that the elderly twin sisters who owned them had intended it purely for their own entertainment. Otherwise, why would they have sent her and Stark into the pen with the contrary animals and cackled when the wily beasts charged and kicked him, only to calmly walk in later with halters, slip them over the animals' heads and lead them into the barn, as docile as lambs—unless Stark came too close.

"What now?" Meri asked.

"Ears," Stark answered, reaching out to hand her the appropriate tool for the examination. Both animals skittered sideways, knocking Meredith on her rump. "Sorry," he muttered.

She got her feet beneath her, stood and

brushed herself off. No wonder he came home some days and showered in his clothes. "Not your fault."

He had told her what to look for, and after scanning photos on the computer earlier, she felt fairly confident that she'd recognize any true anomalies. Then she lifted the first long, droopy ear and didn't even have to shine a light inside.

"Eww."

"Okay, that's got to be cleaned out," Stark decided. "We'll have to sedate her. While I get this ready, you can check the other one." Nodding, Meri slipped the otoscope into her hip pocket and turned to the other goat. While Stark filled a syringe, he muttered, "I ought to get the dart gun."

"You have a dart gun?" she asked as she checked the other goat's ears.

"I do, but I only carry doses for larger animals. If I hit her with one of those, she'd be out for days. Or maybe permanently."

Meri suppressed the urge to laugh. These goats really hated him, and the feeling seemed mutual. "This one's ears seem fine."

The first goat barely twitched when Meredith injected the sedation, but she had to shove the other goat out into the corral before Stark could tend the sedated one. The untreated one ran around, bawling so frantically that the sisters came out to see what was going on.

Standing beside the truck later, she and Stark pulled off their gloves and the overshirts they'd worn because the goats were infuriated by the sight of the brightly colored treatment coveralls. Meredith had again worn her dad's old snap-front flannel, now flecked with paint. Stark's mottled, dark green shirt had been worn thin with washing, and one cuff and the collar were torn. They bundled everything together and tossed it all into the backseat of his truck, then scraped off their boots and dusted down their jeans before climbing into the front.

"Well, here's a new record," Stark said, tapping the digital clock on the instrument panel of his dash. "I believe I might actually have time for lunch today, thanks to my goat wrangler."

Meredith laughed.

"What do you say? It's on me. Can you stomach the diner?"

"I can if you can."

"As long as I don't have to eat goat cheese," he quipped, starting up the engine.

Meredith could hardly believe her ears. Stark Burns was teasing. Would wonders never cease? She had to smile, something very like happiness welling up inside her.

They drove the couple miles into town, laughing about how those goats had chased and charged Stark. "They *really* don't like you," Meredith said again.

"I'm telling you, they don't like men. They hated me the first time I showed up, before I ever laid a finger on them. That's an all-female establishment, and the goats like it that way."

Meri giggled. "How did you manage on your own?"

"I came home bloodied and bruised!" he declared.

She bubbled over with laughter. "But you keep going back."

"Someone has to. No one else to do it."

"You're a nice man, Stark Burns. You don't seem to want anyone to know it, but you're really a very nice man."

"Humph," he said. Then, after a moment, he said, "You were good out there today. You keep a cool head. You follow instructions. And you have sure hands." He cut her a glance, adding, "You handled those man-hating goats well." He grinned, and she laughed.

"Thank you. I feel like I've finally been of real help."

"You've been helpful all along. How are you at bookkeeping?"

She shrugged, trying not to show how hopeful she felt, as if she might really be making a place for herself here. "I can balance a checkbook."

"It's a beginning."

They reached town and drove along Main Street, all two blocks of it, to park in front of the War Bonnet Diner. The place was bustling when they went in, but that didn't mean all the tables were filled. Stark took the table nearest the door. That put them right in the pathway of everyone coming and going. People stopped to ask Meredith about her dad and to say they were praying for him. She gave them all the same report.

"He's feeling better every day and looking more and more like his old self. We're expecting good news in a couple of weeks, and we sure appreciate y'all's prayers."

The pastor of the town church, where her family had attended before she'd left home, was one of those who stopped by to inquire about Wes. Meri rose to hug the middle-aged man, and talk wandered into old times. She couldn't help noticing that he seemed to make Stark uncomfortable. Stark was hunched over his plate and seemed to be trying to ignore everything that was said, whereas he'd quietly joined in with other folks. He'd even told several people that Meredith was working for him now.

As he was taking his leave, the pastor paused and said, "Dr. Burns, good to see you again."

Stark lifted his chin in acknowledgment, but his smile was cool at best. When it became obvious that he wasn't going to speak, Meredith said, "I'm working for Dr. Burns now."

The pastor brightened. "Oh! Does that mean you're staying in War Bonnet?"

"I hope so," she said, glancing at Stark. "I'd like to."

She hadn't officially quit her job at the hospital yet, and the lease wasn't up on her apartment until the end of March, so if things didn't work out at the veterinary clinic, she could always go back to Oklahoma City. She didn't want to, though.

"Your father must be so pleased," the pastor said, smiling. "I know I am."

"Thank you," Meredith told him. "It was good to see you again. Give my best to your wife."

"I will."

He glanced at Stark, his smile fading, and went out.

"That was awkward," Meredith said softly, reclaiming her seat.

Stark shrugged, then sighed. "We've had quite a few...debates. I guess that's the best word."

"Ah."

Stark dropped his fork and wiped his hands. "He was anxious to get me into church when I first came here, and I...wasn't ready for it."

"I see." She steepled her hands over her plate. "Well, maybe you'd be more comfortable attending services at Countryside Church with me and my family then. The atmosphere is very relaxed there. I think that's one of the things Dad likes best."

He picked up his fork again. "I'll think about it."

Meredith rolled her eyes. *Thinking about it* was always his fallback position. "Stark," she said gently, keeping her voice low, "you can't stay mad at God forever."

He left his fork on his plate and laid his hands flat on the table, staring at the food he hadn't eaten yet.

"I don't know how to be anything else," he said, never lifting his gaze from his plate.

Automatically, she reached across the table, laying her hand on top of his. After a moment, he flipped his hand and curled his fingers, interlacing them with hers. Then he picked up his fork with the other hand and finished his meal. He chewed for a long while, swallowed and lifted his glass for a sip of water before carefully wiping his mouth with the paper napkin beside his plate. Finally he sat back, pulling his hand from hers. Only then did he allow their gazes to meet.

Smiling tenderly, he said, "Your lunch is getting cold."

Meredith somehow managed to finish eating.

It wasn't easy with her heart lodged firmly in her throat.

Chapter Eight

He actually considered going to church the next day. Sundays were Stark's one day to sleep in, and he didn't set an alarm. Yet, he'd woken in plenty of time to make the morning service, had he chosen to do so. What had surprised him most was that he'd kind of wanted to go. He kept imagining how pleased Meri would be if he showed up.

Her whole face would brighten, and she'd smile in that beautiful way that made him want to...

Oh, there he went again, thinking of things he had no business thinking. She would not welcome such thoughts, not from any man, especially him. Besides, he had no intention of following through. The very last thing either of them needed in their lives was romance. That's what made this arrangement work.

Wasn't it?

So why had she taken his hand in the diner yesterday? Come to think of it, why had she never shied away from him except for the one time he'd surprised her? Was he wrong about what had happened to her? He thought back, recalling all she'd said on the subject. Several things stood out.

If it hadn't been me that night, it would have been some other woman... He told me to be quiet and let him do what he wanted and he wouldn't hurt me, but I screamed and struggled, so he stabbed me...I wasn't going to let him take anything more than I had to.

A chill shivered through Stark. How easily she could have been killed! If not for that necklace she'd been wearing she could so easily have died. It was bad enough that she had been assaulted, very likely raped.

He closed his eyes, hurting for her. She didn't deserve that. She didn't deserve to live with fear and distrust now or the kind of loneliness that he sometimes sensed in her. He wanted less trauma and more well-being for her, for *every* woman. But every woman did not fall into his orbit. This one did. It was natural that he should feel a tendency to take care of her.

Wasn't it?

Recalling that a short time ago he'd considered her trauma a good reason to hire her, he felt a curling shame, which gave him more reason for prayer. As if a dam had burst, he found himself suddenly in conversation with the God he had ignored—if not railed against—for four long years now. At the end of it, he felt he could stand a little straighter, perhaps taller, than he had since his wife and daughter had died, and for once he didn't hate Sunday quite so much.

He watched a movie that he'd downloaded onto his computer, napped, ate lunch and dinner out of his own private stash of groceries there in the clinic, caught up on his reading and packed his kit for the next day's appointments. When Meredith came in the next morning, he surprised them both by greeting her with a brief hug.

She'd brought that delicious oatmeal for breakfast again. As he watched her unpack the meal, he said, "If you're going to cook for me every morning, why don't you bring enough for the both of us and eat here? Looks like it would be easier. Might even save a little time."

She froze for an instant, then calmly resumed setting out the foodstuffs. "Or," she said, "you could get one of those portable electric burners, and I could cook here."

He had no idea what she was talking about, but he shrugged. "Whatever works."

"You know," she went on carefully, "if you had a lunch kit, I could pack you a lunch to take with you. Then you wouldn't miss so many meals."

He glanced down at her. "Determined to fatten me up, aren't you?"

"More like not let you waste away."

He chuckled and patted her on the back, leaving his hand in place. "It wasn't a complaint."

She shot him a brief smile, not seeming to mind his touch in the least.

He took his hand away and pulled his wallet from his pocket. Extracting a credit card from its leather slot, he tossed it onto the desk. "Buy whatever you need."

"Okay," she quipped, "where's my boss, and what have you done to him?"

He laughed and sat down at the desk. "Your boss has gotten used to good food again." He took her hand in his. "And in case he hasn't said it before, thank you."

She smiled, squeezed his hand and asked, "Want some coffee?"

"Yes, please."

Moving away, she went to the coffeepot, leaving him to wonder if she thought he was harmless because he still grieved his late wife. To his own shock, he was discovering that she would be wrong about that, so wrong that over the next couple days touching her became a game for him.

He never surprised her. That would be cruel and wrong. Nevertheless, he took advantage of every opportunity for contact. While scraping his boots clean at the back door, he'd held on to her shoulder instead of the door frame. The hems of her sleeves frequently needed straightening. While going over the bookkeeping with her, he'd had to brush her hair out of the way in order to look over her shoulder and lean close, bracketing her with his arms, his hands planted on the desktop. He'd found a dozen different ways to touch her, and not once had she protested or seemed uncomfortable. Nor had she made the slightest overture of her own. She hadn't taken his hand again or batted her eyelashes at him or, except for the occasional fleeting smile, really even acknowledged that he'd touched her.

Then, on Wednesday morning, the monthly supply shipment came.

He always made time in his appointment

schedule to put things away. Otherwise, the clinic quickly became impassable and he could never find what he needed when he needed it. This was another chore that Meredith could take over, but first he had to show her how to date the boxes and rotate the older ones from the higher cabinets to the lower ones. That meant getting out the ladder and setting it up in the back hallway. He used a rolling cart to carry the boxes so he didn't have to go up and down the ladder a dozen times. Still, it meant several trips up and down to get everything in place.

"This is one job I will not miss," he told her as she carefully bent to pick up yet another box from the cart. They'd already moved the higher boxes to the lower shelves that had emptied as the month had passed. Frowning at how far she had to bend and noting that she'd hooked her foot around the leg of the ladder in an attempt to stabilize herself, Stark said, "You might have to come down another step."

But she was already toppling headfirst toward the cart. He shoved the cart back and caught her. She landed facedown in his arms, her upper hand clamping around his neck, the other grabbing onto the side of his shirt just above his belt. The ladder went skittering sideways and wound up leaning against the back door on two legs. Lifting her, he brought her up chest to chest, facing him. He could feel her heart hammering in time with his. For a long moment, they stared at each other in shock. Then she just sort of *relaxed*, her arms going around him and her legs bending at the knees.

He was perfectly aware that she was safe and…beautiful, but all the same, he asked, "You okay?"

She smiled at him. "Uh-huh. I wouldn't have been if you hadn't caught me, though."

"You should've come down another step," he said absently, unable to look anywhere except at her lips.

"From now on I will," she promised breathlessly, her lips seeming to come closer with every syllable.

He nodded dumbly, standing there like a lump, with her in his arms, until her smile widened and it occurred to him that he really ought to put her down. When he looked around, though, he saw that the floor was littered with boxes and supplies. He didn't think anything dangerous, like glass, was broken, but just to be safe, he turned and carried her out of there, feeling ten feet tall and as strong as Samson. When he let her feet swing down to the floor, she didn't immediately move away, and that was dangerous. Very dangerous. Reaching behind him, he hung his thumbs in his back pockets to keep from reaching for her again.

"Thank you," she said. "That was quick thinking. I'll be more careful, you can be sure."

He nodded. "Close call."

"Yes. Very." She turned away, but then she abruptly swung back again, mimicking his stance. "Can I ask you something?"

Since the goats, she'd taken to wearing jeans with her scrub tops, a lethal combination to his mind. He managed *not* to clear his throat and still speak nonchalantly. "Sure."

"You remember that Dad's testing to determine the state of his cancer starts tomorrow morning."

"I remember. You'll be off tomorrow and Friday to take him to the hospital in Oklahoma City."

"Yes, and because so much is riding on this, our whole family and a lot of our friends are meeting at our church tonight for a special prayer meeting for Dad. He'll be there, too. I'd like it, and I know he'd like it, if you could join us. Do you think you might?"

Stark couldn't think of a single reason he

could not. He knew such reasons existed and that they were good ones. He'd been using them for four years, after all. At the moment, however, not a single one came to mind, so he just smiled tightly and said, "I can do that."

Meri beamed, bouncing up on her toes. "That's wonderful! Oh, I'm so glad." She told him the time. "You know where Countryside Church is, don't you?"

"I know where it is."

She beamed at him some more. Then she half turned and said, "Well, I'd better clean up the mess I made."

"I'll help you."

"No, no," she protested. "You have appointments. I'll be very careful. Besides, it's my mess. I'll take care of it."

He really had no business putting himself into close proximity with her again, anyway, so he nodded. "I'll go out the front."

"That might be best." She slipped into the back hall, but then she stuck her head out again. "Don't forget your lunch."

"Right." She'd shown up with the new lunch kit and a toaster oven that morning. The electric burner was on order and would arrive soon, along with a few pots and pans.

"See you tonight."

He nodded, shouldered his medical pack,

picked up the lunch she'd packed for him and went out.

What was it about that woman? First she had him praying, and now she had him going to a prayer meeting. Add to that the fact that she'd practically set up housekeeping for him in what had previously been a clinic with a bed, and his life was beginning to approach something that could be considered *normal*.

What was worse was how close he'd come to kissing her just now. And how much he still wanted to do that.

Well aware that Stark hadn't been attending services at any church, Meredith hovered anxiously in the foyer of the small, neat, unpretentious building. She hadn't told her family that he had promised to come, just in case he found an excuse not to. No doubt, he'd intended to come as he'd promised, but after what had happened—or almost happened— that morning, she wouldn't have been surprised if he'd changed his mind. On the other hand, she'd had the feeling lately that he was somehow testing her, trying to figure out if she was interested in him romantically. Unfortunately, she didn't know if he might be developing feelings for her, too, or if he would summarily fire her if she suspected how greatly she was attracted to him. At times, she thought for certain that the attraction was mutual. This morning seemed to prove that it was, but that might be all the reason he needed to let her go. That being the case, she felt great relief when his truck pulled into the graveled parking lot.

She walked out to meet him, pulling her duster-length sweater tighter over the simple black knit top that she wore with jeans and tall black boots. She'd splurged on the boots ages ago and hardly ever wore them. The long lines made her look taller. Besides, she really didn't have a lot from which to choose. Work and fear had curtailed her social life so much that she had neglected her wardrobe shamefully. Come to think of it, she couldn't remember the last time she'd worn lipstick. She hoped the shade that she'd chosen tonight was subtle enough to go without comment.

Stark came around the front of his truck, fitting his good black hat to his head. Freshly shaved, he wore a dark blue tweed sport coat over a white shirt and clean dark jeans, with square-toed black boots.

Sweeping his gaze over her, he said, "You're looking good."

She smiled, fresh relief mixed with delight flowing through her. "Thank you. Nice jacket."

He tugged on his cuffs. "Thanks."

They turned and walked to the building side by side.

"Hey, I've been meaning to ask you something," he said. "I imagine you ride, growing up on a ranch, but I thought I ought to make sure. It could come in handy."

"Of course I ride," Meri answered. "I'm not as comfortable on horseback as Ann and Rex, but I've logged plenty of hours in the saddle. It's been a while, though."

"We'll work on it," he said, "assuming the Straight Arrow can loan us a couple mounts."

"I'm sure that can be arranged."

"Great."

That felt promising. Obviously, he wasn't ready to toss her out on her ear just yet.

They had come to the door, so he reached around her and pulled it open. She stepped through in front of him, then paused to wait for him to catch up to her, feeling his hand on the small of her back, urging her forward. That hand stayed in place as they walked across the foyer and through the double doors into the sanctuary, where Stark swept off his hat. People turned, nodded, gestured. Stark nodded back.

Feeling many eyes on them, Meri did her best not to smile like the cat that ate the canary as they progressed down the aisle, him matching his steps to hers. When they came to the pew where her family sat, she started to gesture for them to make an extra space, but Stark caught her by the elbow and looked pointedly at the pew just behind. A long stretch of space beckoned. She could have sat beside her family with him on his own behind, but she slipped into the empty space with him and lowered herself onto the pew.

Stark sat next to her on the end, his hat in his hands, glancing around as much as he could without turning his head. She knew that he felt uncomfortable, so she patted his knee, thrilled when his big hand covered hers. His eyes mere slits, he gave her the barest smile, and that's all it took to make her heart start pounding.

What was it about him that moved her so? How did he make her feel safe and at the same time excited? She hadn't even liked him a few weeks ago. The man could be positively exasperating and utterly endearing. She was starting to read him, to know what he was feeling and thinking. It scared her a little.

Everything she knew about him told her that he was a bad risk. One wrong step and she could find herself cut out of his life completely, and yet they'd come such a long way already.

He'd allowed her to make changes around the clinic. Even better, he let her take care of him in some ways, and that brought her more pleasure than it probably should. If only he could let go of the guilt and anger surrounding the deaths of his wife and daughter, they might have a chance at something special, something beyond boss and employee, more than mere friendship. Did she dare hope for that, though? Was she even ready for more than friendship?

When she was with him, she thought so. When she wasn't with him, she wondered if she imagined how comfortable she felt with him. How was it even possible to be comfortable and excited with the same man?

Her faith told her that if she really cared for him, she'd be more concerned for him than herself. That being the case, she focused her prayers almost as much on Stark that evening as on her father. Oh, she prayed mightily for her father's healing, silently joining her prayers to those of her family and friends, but she also prayed that Stark would be able to put his guilt and anger behind him and find true healing, spiritually and emotionally.

During the prayer time, Stark sat forward, his elbows braced on his knees, his hat in his hands, his head bowed. Meri sat beside him, her hands folded and eyes closed, wishing she had the courage—and the right—to link her arm with his as Rex and Callie did, while Rex kept his other arm around their dad. Dean sat with his arm wrapped around Ann, their heads together. At one point, Meri leaned forward and touched Ann's shoulder. Ann reached up and grasped her hand, then took Callie's hand on the other side, so all the family were linked to Wes through Rex. To Meri's absolute delight, Stark silently took her other hand.

After the meeting, when everyone rose to leave, several people came to shake Stark's hand. Some of those said, "Glad y'all were here," as if she and Stark were a couple.

Meri couldn't be upset about that. She just smiled and pretended not to notice.

Wes worked his way over to them and clapped Stark on the shoulder. "Thanks for coming, Stark. I appreciate it."

"I want you to have a good report," Stark said.

"Don't see how it can be anything else," Wes told him, smiling. He looked more and more fit. His hair had grown in thicker and snow-white, which made his sky-blue eyes look all the brighter. His color was good, if somewhat paler than in years past, and he was gaining weight almost daily, it seemed. "Thanks for giving Meredith the time off to drive me up to the City."

"No problem."

"There's cereal and milk for your breakfast," she reminded Stark, "and fruit if you want it. And there's lunch meat and bread for sandwiches, and several kinds of snacks."

He chuckled. "I saw the groceries you brought in."

"And don't forget to check your calendar. All your appointments are on it. You'll have to take the calls yourself while I'm gone, of course." She'd considered trying to handle them from the City, but that didn't make sense.

Stark sent Wes a dry look that he then switched to her, his lips twitching. "I did this for a long time without you, Meredith."

She grimaced, feeling foolish. "I know."

"But it's a lot easier *with* you," he admitted softly.

Ridiculously pleased, she went up on tiptoe and kissed his cheek, only realizing when he cleared his throat that she might have chosen a more circumspect moment for that.

"Don't worry," he told her, patting her shoulder. "I'll be fine until you get back."

"I'm sure you will," she said, looking at her toes so he wouldn't see the color in her face.

"Well, you have to leave early in the morning." He nodded a farewell and started up the aisle. "Drive safe."

"See you Saturday," she called.

"Saturday," he echoed, glancing over his shoulder.

She watched him stride toward the door and disappear through it, donning his hat once more, and it occurred to her that she had no reason to worry about her feelings for Stark Burns. It was too late for that.

She was half in love with him already, and she didn't see any way to stop it. Chances were very good that he would break her heart, but maybe she'd leave him better than she'd found him. That was something, wasn't it?

Oh, Lord, let it be. If that's all it can be, I'll settle for that and be glad of it.

She would try, anyway. For Stark's sake.

Chapter Nine

Meri hadn't been part of Stark's daily routine long enough for him to wake up missing her. Still, he woke to the unhappy realization that she wouldn't be in that morning, and the place felt especially empty. To make matters worse, he didn't have a field appointment until late morning, so he had plenty of time to sit around eating the cold cereal she'd bought and speculating about what she was doing. That made Thursday one of the longest days in recorded history.

Stark couldn't help wondering if she was thinking of him. Did she worry that he wouldn't eat properly? Had he imagined that her reaction—or lack of reaction—to his touch was anything other than simple, innocent friendship?

He'd gone over that kiss on the cheek a

thousand times, but he couldn't make it anything more than a kiss on the cheek. In public. In church! In front of her father, no less.

The days after Cathy and Bel had died had melded together into cloudy weeks of agonized grief. He'd hardly been able to tell one day from another. They'd all passed with unbearable sadness. Then suddenly months had disappeared, and he'd had to do something or go insane. He'd been at his parents' home in Tulsa all that time, unable to go back to the place where he and Cathy had built a life together, but he'd had to start somewhere, so he'd bought a new truck with part of the insurance settlement and driven back to Ponca City.

He hadn't been able to even turn into the place he and Cathy had built. Instead, he'd gone to the clinic where he hadn't shown up for months and arranged for his partner to buy him out. By that time, the proposition had come as no surprise. After that, friends had packed up his personal things for him. He'd sent Cathy's and Bel's to her mom. She had dispersed them among the family. He'd sold the ranch—the land, house, furnishings, equipment, livestock and all—without ever setting foot on the property again. Then he'd wandered around the state until he'd found this clinic here in War Bonnet, paid cash for it and halfheartedly settled in.

Moneywise, he'd probably never have to work another day in his life if he didn't want to. But then what would he do? Grieve himself to death? At times in the past, the idea had held a certain appeal, felt almost right. Yet, something in him had continued to strive to survive.

All day, Stark kept thinking about something the pastor at Countryside had said in his short message before the prayers had begun on Wednesday evening. The pastor had said that every Christian's ultimate home was Heaven but that God had created this earth for His children, so we all had a natural affinity for it. The pastor contended that God had intended humankind to live here happily, without the taint of sin, but that the gift of free will had allowed sin to enter the picture, so God had always been ready with an alternate plan in the form of Christ. God was always ready with alternate plans, the pastor had said, because this world required them. According to him, we could not always see the wisdom of God's decisions or how they affected everyone involved, but we could always trust that God had everyone's best interests at heart.

Stark had some difficulty with that last statement. In whose best interest was the death of his daughter? He could accept the idea that she and Cathy had passed into Heaven and were happy there now, but how did that benefit anyone else? The very idea angered him.

On the other hand, he couldn't quite find it in him to resent the idea of an alternate plan now that they were gone, though he knew that not long ago he would have. That troubled him, almost as much as how he missed Meredith. Disgusted with himself, he determined to put her out of his mind.

Friday was twice as busy as Thursday, and that should've helped, but somehow it didn't. Despite not having time to take more than two bites out of the sandwich he'd packed for lunch, he couldn't help thinking of Meri. The sandwich didn't taste right, anyway. He'd put everything on it that Meredith had, right down to the salt and pepper, but it just didn't taste the same, which probably meant that he had finally crossed over into certifiably wacko, as did the growing conviction that he'd return to the clinic that evening and find her there, waiting for him.

All that awaited him at the clinic that evening, however, was the electric burner she'd ordered, and a small box of pots and pans to use with it.

He had to fight not to call her. Surely she'd want to know that the burner and pans had arrived, but he knew that if he spoke to her, he'd give himself away. He sat on the edge of his bed with his phone in his hand for a good hour, trying to think how he might word his call and pitch his voice so as not to betray himself for the lonely, heartsick fool he'd become.

It made no sense. He'd avoided as much human contact as he possibly could for four long years, and now he was crushing like mad on his pretty little assistant, who probably didn't even really like him. He'd given her no reason to be interested in him. He no longer even knew how to attract a woman. He was scared to death by even the thought of it.

Tossing the phone onto the bed, he closed his eyes and put his hands to his head. "Oh, God," he prayed aloud, "I don't know how to do this anymore. I think I've forgotten how to live. I know I've forgotten how to trust. Or hope. I'm a mess. Why would any woman want me?"

He sighed, just sitting there in the silence that was his life, and in the back of his mind, he heard a little girl giggle. For the first time in so long he almost couldn't remember how long, he smiled at the memory. Suddenly, memories came at him so fast that he couldn't process them, some happy, some irritating, some just...life. So many hurled themselves at him that he didn't know what to do with them. Desperate to turn them off, he got up and went to his computer, clicking on a television program he'd downloaded and never taken the time to watch.

In the midst of it, he recalled another point the pastor had made on Wednesday evening.

"We all have so much to be thankful for," the pastor had said, "that sometimes we're reluctant to ask for what we want or even need, but God wants, expects, us to come to Him. First in gratitude, yes, but also in petition."

At the time, the words had struck Stark as ridiculous. What did he have to thank God for? Now the thought hit Stark that he'd never really thanked God for Cathy and Belinda and all they'd meant to him, and he certainly hadn't thanked God for surviving the wreck or finding this place or *anything*. He hadn't felt grateful, even when life had been very good. Not until...not until Meredith.

Oh, this was bad. And good. Because it meant he was coming back to life. Which was bad. Except, it could be good. Maybe.

That *maybe* scared the daylights out of him.

What if he let himself love her and she walked away?

What if he let himself love her and something awful happened to her, too?

What if he just *thought* he loved her and it turned out that he really didn't? That he couldn't?

He wondered if he could stop what was happening between them, what he was feeling. But did he want to stop it? He didn't even know anymore. All he seemed able to do now was just go forward one step at a time and *hope*.

Had hope always been this terrifying?

All he knew for sure was that he had to start doing something different or find a way to crawl back into the dark hole that had been his life before he'd hired Meredith Billings. He thought about firing her, but just imagining the look of disappointment on her face tore him up inside. So, forward it was, forward in gratitude.

Sighing, he bowed his head again. He *hoped* reluctant thanks counted because that was all he had to give at the moment.

"Cathy was a perfect wife," he said. Okay, she hadn't been perfect. If she had, she wouldn't have been with him. "She was a good wife, a very good wife. And Bel was a wonderful child. I loved them, and they loved me. We were happy. I miss them." He gulped down the anger that threatened to rise up, and said, "Thank You for all the good years we had together. Thank You that they didn't suffer. Thank You for this place and...for getting me through, I guess. That's all for now. I hope it's enough."

The relief he felt couldn't be qualified. He almost resented it because it felt like letting go of Cathy and Bel. But Cathy and Bel weren't here. They belonged to Heaven now. A rush of tears surprised him. He wiped them away and let himself relax, really relax. Stretching out on the bed, he went to sleep fully clothed and dreamed that Cathy came to the clinic.

"I finally found you," she said. "How are you? Everything okay?"

He was overjoyed to see her. At first. Then he thought, If Cathy's alive, what about Meredith?

As if reading his mind, Cathy smiled and said, "It's all right. Everything in its own time."

"Where's Bel?" he asked. "I want to see her."

But Cathy ignored that or didn't hear it. In that infuriating, puzzling way of dreams, she said, "You should get some horses. Horses are your favorite. Everything in its place."

Then she was gone, and he thought to himself, I really need to sleep more.

He woke well rested the next morning to the happy knowledge that Meri would soon be there.

After unlocking both of the outer clinic doors, he broke out that fancy electric burner and found that it could be dialed to any temperature. Placing it atop the old dresser in his room, he arranged the pans on a small set of rickety shelves that stood next to the refrigerator. Meri had brought in some paper plates and bowls for him, but the pots and pans would have to be washed in the utility sink in the back room. He made a mental note to get a dish drainer, then he washed and dried a skillet and found the bacon that Meri had stashed in the fridge, reasoning that even if she carried in breakfast that morning, bacon wouldn't go amiss. He had that fried up, coffee percolating and hot water for her tea waiting when he heard her car drive in.

Opening the back door before she could try the lock, he let in a blast of chilly air. She greeted him with a smile. He returned the smile with one of his own and a question.

"How'd it go?"

He backed up, giving her room to enter. His arms gave him trouble. He wanted desperately to sweep her into a hug, but he quelled the urge by parking his hands at his waist. She surprised him by walking straight into him, her arms sliding through his and around his chest. What could he do but wrap her up and squeeze her tightly, puffy coat, handbag and all?

"It's good news."

He briefly closed his eyes. "Thank You, God." He almost chuckled. Looked like he was forming some new habits.

She pulled back then, adjusting the strap of her handbag on her shoulder. Her smile said it all. "We'll have to wait for the report to filter through Dr. Shorter's office here in town, but the preliminary news is excellent."

Cupping her cheek with his hand, he said, "I am so glad."

She nestled her cheek against his palm, her smile broadening. Then she sniffed and asked, "Is that bacon?"

He nodded. "Everything came. That burner's something. Come see."

Catching her hand, he turned down the hall and led her into the clinic proper. She dropped his hand to sling off her coat and hang it up in the corner. Stashing her handbag in a cubby above the reception desk, she said, "I brought French toast to cook in the toaster oven. It's out in the car."

"French toast and bacon," he said, grinning. "Yum."

She started toward him, but just then a woman burst through the front door into the waiting area, calling, "Doc Burns!"

He recognized the elderly woman at once and hurried forward to take the box that she carried. Balancing it on the edge of the reception desk, he looked down at the bloody feathers, sighed and shook his head. Not again.

"Supper!" he scolded.

Feeling a sharp slap on his upper arm, he looked over at Meri, who glared, inclining her head at the rooster's owner. A moment passed before Stark realized the problem, but then he bit back a grin.

"Supper is the rooster's name."

Clearly, Meredith had thought he was giving up on the bird and had pronounced it fit only for the dinner table. Her lovely mouth formed a sweet O.

"You'll find his records under the name of Kate Miriam."

Meri grit her teeth in an apologetic grimace, which she kept carefully hidden from Ms. Miriam. "I see."

Stark did his best to maintain a properly stoic countenance. "If you'd bring those records to Exam One, we'll see what we can do for Supper."

"Yes, sir. At once."

"Have a seat, Ms. Miriam," he said to the older woman. "We'll be as quick as we can."

"Thank you so much," the old lady warbled tearfully. "Dumb bird just won't leave that cat alone."

"Looks like he'd learn," Stark said, carrying the box toward the exam room.

"Hasn't so far," Kate Miriam grumbled in a worried tone.

Meri smoothly offered the distraught woman coffee, then joined Stark in the treatment room. She glanced over the lengthy file as Stark outfitted himself to administer treatment and Supper poked his head up over the edge of the box, clucking and looking around.

"Is he in shock?"

"Partly," Stark answered, gently handling the rooster inside the box. "Mostly he's just tame."

Meri continued to peruse the file. "How many times have you patched up this bird?"

"Lost count. He and the neighbor's cat that he tussles with practically pay the bills around here."

"Why does she let him out of the henhouse?"

"He doesn't have a henhouse," Stark said with a chuckle. "He's not equipped for a henhouse. He was headed for the stew pot on her brother's farm when Kate rescued him and decided to keep him for a pet. He has a doghouse, and all would be well except that Supper likes to peck through the fence at the neighbor's cat, so occasionally the cat comes calling. Then it's World War Three, and somebody winds up in here. I keep telling them to board up the fence or enclose that rooster house, but nobody listens to me. We're going to need some stitches." He told Meredith what was required and started cleaning the wounds while she went for the correct medications and laid out sutures.

Supper knew the drill and hardly ruffled his feathers while Stark worked. Once the bird was sedated, Stark lifted him out of the box and onto a sterile sheet to complete the treatment. The old rooster was going to be missing some feathers, but what were a few more at this point? After the stitching and all the little nicks and cuts were addressed, they lined the box with another sterile sheet, laid the snoozing rooster back in the box and carried him outside with a bottle of antibiotic capsules and an empty syringe. Stark gave instructions to Ms. Miriam, who by now likely knew exactly how to open the capsules, dissolve the antibiotic powder in a syringe of water and shoot it down Supper's throat.

"I can't pay you till the first," she began, but Stark waved away her concern.

"We'll bill you, and, like always, you can pay it out."

She smiled. "Thank you, Dr. Burns." Petting the rooster's feathered head, she muttered, "Dumb bird," but she hugged the box tightly as she carried it out of there.

As the door shut behind her, Stark said, "That's got to be the most expensive rooster that ever lived."

Meri snickered, and then they were both laughing.

"She clearly loves the thing," Meri said when she'd finally calmed enough to speak.

"Why do you think I keep patching it up?"

"I'm s-sorry," Meri spluttered, launching into fresh gales of mirth, "but when you c-called it S-Supper, I thought—"

"I know what you thought." He chuckled, tears coming to his eyes. "You thought I was telling her to cook it, eat it and be done with it."

"S-Supper." She giggled. "What a name!"

He'd never had anyone to share this with

before Meredith. It felt good to laugh about something as silly as a rooster named Supper.

In fact, life felt pretty good right now—and downright scary, especially if it meant that he was falling in love. The thought of loving again terrified him, but the life he'd been living didn't pay homage to anyone, least of all the last woman he'd loved.

What was the point of living at all if he couldn't be man enough to face down his fears, to take a new risk?

Sobering, he blew out a breath and caught Meri by the hand. He tried to think how to say it, how to tell her what he wanted. In the end, he just looked her in the eye and put it as straight as he knew how.

"I really want to kiss you."

She stepped closer, turned up her face and softly said, "Please do."

His hand shook as he again lightly cupped her cheek. Her eyelashes, a rosy shade of gold, sparkled with the tears she'd shed in her laughter. Eyes like ovals plucked from a clear sky smiled up at him. She had a perfect nose, skin like porcelain, the whitest teeth and wide, plump, pink lips. Such beauty. Had he really ignored this in the beginning?

It had been so long since he'd kissed a woman, but he couldn't remember ever wanting a kiss more. Bending his head, he gently pressed his lips to hers and felt the tiny quakes in them that might have been nerves or enjoyment on her part. Mindful of all she'd been through, unwilling to frighten or threaten her in any way, he kept every touch as gentle as possible.

Then she thrilled him when her arms slid around his waist. He settled his hands on her slender shoulders before sliding them down to cover her back. She felt so small, so petite, but so womanly. For the first time in far too long he felt like a whole man.

The phone rang, pulling them apart. Meredith turned her head, looking to the desk.

"So much for breakfast."

"I still have a little while yet," he said softly, moving toward the desk. "You tend to breakfast. I'll get the phone."

Nodding, she reached for her coat at the same time Stark reached for the phone.

"War Bonnet Veterinary," he said into the mouthpiece, watching her head out to her car for the breakfast makings. He listened with one ear to the farmer on the end of the line while his mind churned with other possibilities.

He knew now that it wasn't all in his fevered mind. She felt it, too, this thing growing between them. So, he had a decision to make. He just wasn't sure that he had the courage to choose what he really wanted. A second loss would destroy him. He'd thought the first one had. How could he love another woman and face the prospect of losing her?

It was one thing to feel like this, another to lose the source of those feelings. He wasn't sure he could do it. He wasn't sure he *should* do it.

Yet, that moment when her arms had come around him while he kissed her was going to stay with him forever.

Maybe that was all he was meant to have. Either way, he would be sure to thank God for it.

The day seemed made for dreaming. Stark's little room was becoming crowded with all the kitchen goods she'd encouraged him to bring in, but at least he was beginning to live like a normal human being. And that kiss! She hadn't imagined the pull between them or the little ways in which he touched her. He was laughing more, too, and he hadn't been angry in days. She hadn't realized before how kind and caring he could be, even with ridiculous old roosters that picked fights with cats and the softhearted old ladies who loved them.

She wondered if he realized that he'd kissed her cheek as he'd rushed out that morning, still munching bacon.

Tingling with possibilities, she shamelessly indulged in all sorts of daydreams: her and Stark driving into Ardmore for movies, to the lake for picnics, over to the houses of friends and family for parties, sitting together in church, working together like a perfectly functioning team, kissing and holding each other tight. She felt seventeen again, but this time the boy she liked actually noticed her.

To make her world a perfect place, her father's tests had shown no discernible cancer. Meredith felt as if she could truly breathe again, as if the world was once more rife with hope and possibility. It would take time, of course. Five years of such tests must pass before her dad could be pronounced cured, but why be discouraged? She didn't kid herself that Stark was ready for anything more than dating at this point, either.

In the end, he just might decide that she wasn't the girl for him. Being the woman in whom he was interested now and the woman with whom he ultimately wound up were two very different propositions. Besides, she had determined to think of what was best for *him* and trust God to take care of her. She could hope, though, and she did.

How could she feel his hand on her face and the power of his kiss and not hope? She allowed herself to dream that hope all the way up to quitting time. Then she switched the call forwarding to Stark's cell phone and locked the doors.

Just as she reached for her coat, though, the phone rang. She waited for Stark to pick up, in case he then had instructions for her. Better to take them here than on the road. He didn't pick up the call, though. Instead, it went to voice mail, which rerouted it back to the office phone. She saw the light come on the console and rushed over to snatch up the receiver, cutting off the recorded message.

"This is Meredith at War Bonnet Veterinary Services. How can I help you?"

"Meredith did you say?" a man's voice asked with obvious surprise.

"Yes, sir. How may I help?"

"Is this an answering service by chance?"

"No, sir. I'm Dr. Burns's assistant."

"Really?" Now the man sounded downright chipper. "Meredith, you've just made my day. This is Dr. Burns's father. Perhaps you have a moment to talk."

Chapter Ten

Dropping down onto the desk chair, Meredith tried to recall what Stark had said about his family. Not much. There had been something about a monthlong Thanksgiving tradition and his father being a coach. She remembered that he had two sisters and a brother, all younger than him, and that he was originally from Tulsa, which was where the accident had occurred that had taken the lives of his wife and daughter. That was about it. She certainly didn't remember anything negative or hurtful about them.

"I guess that would be all right," she said in reply to Stark's father's request for conversation.

The man on the other end of the telephone line introduced himself as Marvin Burns.

"My wife, Andi, and I didn't even know Stark had hired help."

"Yes, sir. I've been here a few weeks."

"I'd say that's a step in the right direction. Maybe Stark will at least get our messages now."

"Absolutely."

"To tell you the truth," Marvin Burns said, "I suspect he's been getting them all along. He just ignores them."

"Oh, I'm sure that's not so," Meri lied smoothly, quite sure that Marvin Burns was right. "Stark, er, Dr. Burns is very busy, you know. Very busy."

"Hmm. I don't doubt it. Too busy for church or friends, I imagine."

Meredith winced, hearing the concern in the man's voice, and said the first thing that came into her head. "Actually, he was in church on Wednesday night."

"Really? Better and better. Tell me, is he seeing anyone?"

"Uh…"

"Too personal. My apologies. Maybe you could just tell me who his friends are. Or if he has friends. We can't help worrying that he spends all his off time alone."

"Of course he has friends," Meredith said, hoping to allay as much of his parents' worry as possible. "My brother and father think very highly of S—your son. Everyone around here does."

"I see. That's good to hear. Would you happen to know where he's been spending his holidays? Because he hasn't been home, really been home, in years. He hasn't spent a total of eight hours here in over three years."

In other words, Stark had barely seen his parents since coming to War Bonnet.

Meredith pinched the bridge of her nose to keep tears at bay. Knowing Stark, he'd spent every holiday right here in that Spartan little room of his, all alone, but his parents didn't need to know that.

"I really couldn't say for sure, Mr. Burns. I'm sorry."

"You've no idea how much his mother and I would love to see him for Thanksgiving or Christmas this year," the older man said. "It would mean the world to us, Meredith."

"I understand. I've only recently come home myself because my father's been ill."

"I am sorry. I hope it's not serious."

"It has been, but he's much improved. The last report was a very good one. Stark came to church to pray for him before his tests." She didn't bother about using Stark's given name this time. Marvin Burns needed to know that his son had people around him who cared about him.

"Now that," said his father, "does my heart a great deal of good. Thank you for telling me."

"I'll make sure he gets this message," she promised, "and I'll do all I can to make sure that he's not alone for the holidays this year, at the very least."

"Bless you, my dear. Bless you. Do you mind if I ask your last name?"

"It's Billings. Meredith Billings."

"I'll be praying for your father's continued good health."

"Thank you so much, and goodbye."

"Goodbye."

Meredith hung up the phone and sat staring at it for several long seconds. So much for daydreams.

How could Stark have failed to spend even a few days with his parents in the past three years and more? They weren't at fault in the deaths of his wife and daughter. The only person who could have been assigned any fault had died in the same accident. Why couldn't Stark see that? Shutting everyone out of his life had to stop. Otherwise, Stark had no life, not really. He just couldn't go on ignoring his parents, refusing to take their phone calls, ignoring their messages.

Of course, when she delivered *that* message, he was likely to shut *her* out of his life, but she had to at least try. For his sake.

She decided that this was too important to put off until Monday morning. This needed to be handled as soon as possible. After calling home to say that she didn't know what time she'd be in, she took the whole thing to God. Once she'd prayed herself out, she got up to pace.

Eventually, she sat down on one of the padded chairs in the waiting area to read, but she soon worked her way through all the available material. Stark really needed to get in some fresh magazines. She thought she'd catnap for a bit, think what to say to Stark when he came in, rest her eyes...

"Meri? Babe?" The voice in her head seemed to come to her down a long tunnel, but the hand on her shoulder felt very real. "You okay? What's wrong?"

Stirred to wakefulness, she sat up, sucking in a deep breath. "I guess I fell asleep. Talking to your dad."

"You fell asleep. Talking to my dad?"

Blinking, she focused her eyes. Stark crouched in front of her, a towel wrapped around his shoulders. He was wet, from his head to his bare feet.

"You showered in your clothes again."

"Had to. I was filthy. What's this about my father?"

"He telephoned. They miss you, Stark. Your mom and dad miss you."

"Oh, is that all," he said, sighing and hanging his head. "Scared me half to death seeing you there like that."

"What do you mean is that all?" she scolded, frowning.

"I thought something was wrong with you," he explained, glaring at her. "I didn't mean that it's nothing. I just meant..." He stroked a hand through her hair. "I'm glad there's nothing wrong with you."

"There *is* something wrong with me," she said, trying not to be swayed by the thrill of his touch. "You are hurting your parents. They need to talk to you, to see you. You won't always have them, Stark. I know. My mom's already gone, and my dad could have died at any time this past year."

"You don't have to tell me about death, Meredith." He folded his arms in a gesture very reminiscent of the old Stark, and that brought out the old Meri.

"The point is, you didn't bury the whole

world when you buried your wife and daughter," she snapped. She thought for a moment that he would blow up at her, and that she could have put that more gently. "I'm sorry," she said. "That was an ugly thing to say. It's just that you still have family who love you, and I don't want you to waste that."

After a few seconds he nodded. "You're right. Can you let me get into some dry clothes before we talk more about it?"

"Of course," she answered softly.

He went into the bedroom, then came out again seconds later, carrying a stack of clean clothing. He walked to the far back corner of the building, and she heard the door to the utility room close. After a minute or two the very faint sound of water running could be heard. She assumed that he'd changed and put his wet, soiled clothing into the washer. He returned a few moments later wearing clean dry jeans, a long-sleeved shirt and heavy socks, combing his hair as he walked. He slipped the comb into his back pocket and sat down across from her.

"Look," he said, "I want to see my parents. The problem, frankly, is my sisters. They're both married with kids, and it's really tough for me to be around that. I'm happy for them, and I want them to be happy, but when I'm around them, all I feel is…like I don't belong anymore." He shook his head. "It's too painful."

Meredith sighed. "I can understand that. Now that my brother and sister are both married, I feel like a fifth wheel. Everyone else is paired up, all billing and cooing, and there I am, pretending not to notice."

Stark nodded. "Your dad must be feeling some of that, too, then."

She shrugged. "I don't know. Maybe. He and Rex and Ann were always pretty close, though, while I was closer to Mom. Now, I kind of feel like Dad and I are closer than before, so maybe it's something we have in common."

"He brags on you," Stark told her, and she couldn't help smiling about that.

"He does?"

"Oh, yeah. He loves all his children. That's easy to see, and I think he's pretty pleased about Rex's and Ann's situations. But he's really glad you've come home, Meri. Given what you've told me, I wonder if he expected it."

"Maybe not, but I'm glad if he's happy about it."

"I'm sure he is."

"Your dad would be pleased if you just went home to visit."

"I know, and I'll try to do that as soon as I can."

"Maybe for Thanksgiving?"

Stark grimaced. "I just don't know if I can handle that, with all the rest of the family there. But I'll call him and arrange something."

"Don't put it off, Stark. Call tonight."

"I will. About Thanksgiving, though." He drummed his thumbs against his thighs. "Maybe you and I could, you know, sort of support each other through the holidays."

She smiled. "That's a thought. Maybe you could spend Thanksgiving with me and my family. Of course, there will still be married couples and children there."

"But they won't be people who knew my late wife and daughter," he said softly, "people I saw them with and remember them with."

"That's true."

"It might be a good way to...reintegrate."

"Okay. So you can tell your dad that you're spending Thanksgiving with the Billings family," she said. "You might be more comfortable with the whole idea if you sort of ease into it. Say, by joining the family for church tomorrow?"

Tilting his head, he flattened his lip as if trying not to smile. "Walked right into that one, didn't I?"

"Uh-huh."

"And you're going to keep right on pushing and pushing and pushing, aren't you?"

"Until you stop me."

He pulled in a very deep breath through his nostrils. Then he got up, spread his hands and said, "See you tomorrow."

All but bursting with delight, Meredith bounced up out of her chair and went for her coat. "Ten thirty, then."

"Yes, ma'am."

"Don't forget to call your dad."

"Uh, yes, ma'am."

"And eat a good dinner."

"Yes. Ma'am. Anything else? Ma'am."

Grinning, she waggled her fingers at him in farewell. "Sleep well."

"Maybe," he muttered.

She didn't want to know what or who he feared might disturb his sleep. If it was his conversation with his dad, he might blame her. If it was thoughts of his late wife or her, both felt equally dangerous.

She was in the car headed home before she realized, happily, that he had called her *babe*.

To Meri's surprise, Sunday felt a little awkward. Maybe it was because she couldn't forget that Stark had kissed her and later called her *babe*. Or maybe it was that Stark had never looked so handsome to her. He wore a black suit coat with his dark jeans and a navy string tie with his white shirt. She realized he'd put on a little weight, mostly in the upper chest and shoulders, and he suddenly looked like a powerhouse, standing there under that high-crowned black beaver cowboy hat, all clean shaven and finely turned out. Altogether, he was more than enough to make a girl's heart go pitter-patter, and she figured hers couldn't be the only one tripping at double time. She *was* the only one his warm brown eyes targeted, though, when he stepped into the foyer of the church building that blustery Sunday of Thanksgiving week.

She'd tried not to be too conspicuous, hanging around and chatting with friends while she'd waited for him to show up. Like him, she'd taken care with her appearance, choosing a long, slim black knit sleeveless dress and a cropped, coral-pink sweater with long sleeves to wear with her best black heels.

She'd rolled her hair into a simple but classy bun low on the back of her head, leaving strands to waft about her face, then donned a pair of heavy turquoise earrings and a matching bracelet that she'd inherited from her mom. She'd applied lipstick and even a little mascara.

Stark made his way through the crowded vestibule straight to her side. He bent and spoke softly into her ear.

"I think you're more beautiful every time I see you."

She almost kissed him then and there. If someone hadn't jostled her, murmuring apologies, she might have. Blushing so hotly her face hurt, she said, half-teasingly, "You certainly pick your moments!"

Glancing around them, he muttered, "A man has to, if he knows what's good for him."

"Do you?" she asked warily, sensing his sudden unease.

"What?"

"Know what's good for you?"

"I doubt it," he answered drily. "Frankly, I've been trusting you for that."

She lifted an eyebrow, hoping no one else was listening to their conversation. "I'm not sure I understand." Or maybe she did. Maybe he'd counted on her to be the one with good sense. After all, he'd been a married man and now had been alone for a long time, and she'd let him kiss her with apparent eagerness. Her blush deepened.

"Hanged if I can figure it out," he muttered, shifting uneasily.

She resisted the urge to rush away and leave him standing there. "We'd best find our seats."

"Lead the way," he agreed, bending his head and palming the crown of his hat. When he straightened, the hat remained in his hand.

This time, being forewarned, the family had left adequate space, so Meri couldn't very well take Stark to a different pew. They sat with everyone else, Wes on one end, Stark on the other. They made a full row of Billings family. And Stark. Greetings rippled down the row, beginning with Dean on Meri's right.

"Hey, man."

"Hello."

"Glad you could come."

"Man, you clean up real good." That was Rex, and Stark rolled his eyes at him.

Wes said, "Well, we're all here. That makes it a red-letter day." As if Stark were a part of the family who had been missing.

Stark smiled stiffly, nodded, cleared his throat and seemed to have a little trouble settling in. He crossed his legs, uncrossed them, laid his arm along the back of the pew behind Meredith, then abruptly took it down again. He shifted his hat from one hand to the other and finally hung it on the corner of the pew in front of him. She wanted to take his hand or slip her arm through his to reassure him, but that suddenly seemed like a terribly personal display in a very public place, and she didn't want him to think that she was inviting intimacies he didn't want or deemed unwise.

After a moment, he whispered out of the corner of his mouth, "I feel like a rooster in a room full of cats."

That made Meredith smile. She had to cover her mouth with a hand to curtail the urge to giggle before she could say, "How do you know how a rooster in a room full of cats feels?"

"I'm an experienced veterinarian," he said in a soft, droning, deadpan voice. "I know these things in-*stinc*-tively."

The way he said "in-*stinc*-tively" cracked her up. She clapped a hand over her mouth to stifle her laughter, tears filling her eyes, shoulders shaking. Who knew Stark could be so funny? She glanced at him, saw the satisfied little curve of his lips and knew that he'd done it on purpose.

Dean elbowed her. "What are you two laughing about?"

Swallowing the mirth, she mastered her other emotions well enough to get out, "Veterinarian joke."

"Yeah? Tell."

She shook her head but then began to explain. "There's this rooster named Supper, and when his owner first brought him in, and Stark said his name, I thought—" Stark snickered, and that set her off in sputters so she couldn't say more. Thankfully, the music started so she had no time to try again.

Later, she noticed that Stark wasn't singing. He just stood there with his hands folded, nodding along in time to the music. She went up on tiptoe and said into his ear, "How come you're not singing? Don't you know these songs?"

He bent down and answered, "I know them, but you don't want me even trying to sing. Trust me. Singing is not my talent."

"Can't be that bad," she said, looking up at him.

He bent down again. "Babe, if singing was the only requirement for getting into Heaven, those pearly gates would close right in my face."

Babe again. Why did that one little word

make her go weak in the knees? This time she curled her arm around his. "When you get there, I'm sure you'll do just fine."

He said nothing to that, but when they sat down again, he wrapped his hand around the bracelet on her arm and kept it there. She noticed that he paid particular attention to the sermon, but his hand didn't leave her arm until they rose again.

At the end of the service, he took his hat and stepped out into the aisle, seeming quietly thoughtful. People moved past and around him, but he paid no attention. His mind was obviously elsewhere. When Meri laid her hand in the bend of his elbow, he looked around as if he'd forgotten where he was for a moment.

"You're welcome to join us for Sunday dinner," she said.

"Please do, Stark," Callie said, appearing at his shoulder. "There's always plenty."

He was already shaking his head, though. "Y'all feed me enough already," he said, "and I thank you."

"Are you sure you won't change your mind?" Wes asked, but Stark was firm.

"No, sir, not this time. Thanks all the same. I'm going to want to talk to you about buying some horses, though, sometime in the next couple weeks, maybe."

"Oh? You buying or selling?"

"Buying. Thinking on it, anyway. Been a long time since I had my own riding stock. No one around here has better horses than Straight Arrow, so I thought you might know where I should start looking."

"I've got some ideas," Wes said, obviously pleased.

"Knew you would." He looked at Meredith then. "Meri, a word?"

"Of course."

He waved his hat in farewell to the others, and they walked up the aisle side by side, speaking briefly to everyone who spoke to them. In the foyer, he ushered her into a quiet corner.

"I wanted to tell you that there's no need for you to come in tomorrow until after your dad's appointment with Dr. Shorter. I know it's early, and I know it's important. I also know that he depends on you to interpret the medical lingo for him."

She smiled at his thoughtfulness but said, "I can come in as usual and just meet Dad at Dr. Shorter's."

"That's not necessary."

"But your breakfast—"

"I can feed myself," he interrupted, looking down at the hat in his hands. "You've made sure of that. There's nothing pressing in the morning. I've already called and moved everything to the afternoon. So you go with your dad and come in after. That's an order."

"Okay. If you'll tell me why you won't come to dinner."

He glanced around, bowed his head and finally looked her in the eye. "It isn't safe."

"What?"

"Babe, the way I feel about you scares me like nothing else ever has. And after what happened to you, it should scare you, too."

"That's—" Before she could say *crazy*, he lifted his hand and lightly brushed two fingers over the scar on her chest. She realized suddenly what he must think, what he must assume.

"I'm not even sure you should be working for me anymore."

"Stark, don't say that."

"I mean it. I've thought long and hard about this, and I'm just not sure it's best for either of us. Especially you. I don't know how much longer I can…just be your friend, let alone your boss."

"Stark, we have to talk about this," she whispered urgently. "I think you may have the wrong impression. We need to talk. Promise me."

He nodded. "Yeah. You're right. We'll talk. As much as you're comfortable talking." He cupped her cheek with his big, gentle hand, regret in his dark eyes. Then he shook his head, turned and walked away.

Stunned, Meredith put her head back and looked at the ceiling, sending up a silent prayer.

Please, God, don't let him make a decision without all the facts. Don't let him push me away until I've had my say. For both our sakes.

Chapter Eleven

Why couldn't he be smart about this?

Stark asked himself that question for the umpteenth time, and the only honest answer he could come up with was pure selfishness. Meredith made him feel alive again, but he knew that if he kept on seeing her every day things were going to change, intensify, fly out of control. And that would be bad.

She trusted him not to hurt her, but his affection for her grew daily, and he feared frightening her. She'd likely never get over it if that happened. No doubt she'd run for the hills. Those two reactions together would cut him up inside as bad as Cathy's death, if not worse, which meant they'd both lose.

The only wise choice was to stop it now, before it was too late.

When he'd seen her sleeping on those

chairs in the waiting area of his clinic, he'd wanted to scoop her up and keep her with him, protecting her for the rest of his life. Only later had the impossibility of that hit him. In the moment, he hadn't let himself think through what he was doing or saying, let alone intending.

They could be each other's *support* through the holidays.

He was going to ease into her family by attending church with them.

What he hadn't let on was that he'd already been planning how he was going to introduce her to *his* family. What she hadn't realized was that he was already dreaming about how they'd make new memories, a new life. Together.

That's when the ugly, selfish truth had clobbered him. Considering all she'd been through, he couldn't plan a life with Meredith. It was all sweetness and light right now, but it wouldn't stay that way. He couldn't go on just being her friend forever, and when she realized that, she'd hate him. At the very least, she'd feel betrayed, and she might even be *afraid* of him. After all she'd been through, how could it be any other way?

It was probably best this way. Neither of them was ready for a real relationship. He couldn't get over Cathy, and Meri could never think of him as anything more than a job and an improvement project. He had to face that fact now, before it was too late, before he damaged both of them irreparably.

The realization left him feeling both relieved and deeply burdened. He reasoned that the sooner he dealt with the issue, the better for both of them. Now that her father seemed firmly on the mend, he had no good excuse for putting it off. His feelings would wane over time, become bearable, something he could live with; he knew that from experience.

Surely it was best just to be honest about it. She'd helped him make great strides in the quality of his life, but it had to end there, for everyone's sake. He told himself he'd mourn the loss of his foolish dreams later, but the loss would be tempered by the sure knowledge that what he was doing was best and right for both of them, especially her.

He'd get over it and be the better for it. And so would she. Before long they'd both feel a little silly about the whole thing. They might even be able to go on being friends. He'd continue to work on his issues and she'd continue to work on hers. But apart. Safely apart.

Surely he'd start to feel some peace about

this, some satisfaction with his life as it was now. Without her. This...*bleakness* would pass.

Please, God, let it pass.

He'd grown used to the spurts of delight that she'd brought into his life, the laughter and comfort, the affection. How he would miss her smile and her warmth, but he couldn't afford to weaken. The possibility of disaster was just too high.

He purposefully did not meet her at the door when she finally came in on Monday morning. In fact, he made certain that he was at the desk going over the books on the computer. She called out his name, and the shock of it sent shivers through him.

"Stark?"

"In here."

She breezed in, hung up her outerwear and came straight to him. He could feel her good mood but kept his eyes glued to the computer screen. Perhaps he should have expected what happened next. She walked up behind him, slid her arms around his shoulders, bent forward, laid her cheek atop his head and hugged him. Closing his eyes, he savored every instant of the contact. It might well be the last. Then he caught the break in her breathing and realized she was on the point of tears.

Reacting without prior thought, he rotated the chair, came to his feet and reached for her. "Babe? What's wrong?"

She shook her head, tears glistening in her beautiful blue eyes, her hands on his shoulders. "It's all good," she squeaked, obviously struggling to master her emotions. "Even better than we'd hoped. Oh, Stark, I'm so happy!"

Going up on tiptoe, she hugged him again. He let out his breath in a whoosh of air, relief sweeping through him. "You had me worried."

She went down on her heels, keeping her arms about his neck and laying her head in the hollow of his shoulder. "I railed at God when Dad was first diagnosed," she admitted, sniffing. "I knew how bad it could be, you see. I didn't even tell the others, not until we had a better idea what we were dealing with. Then I thanked God that it wasn't worse and started praying for Dad's complete healing. Now..." She put her head back and looked up at him. "Now I realize that Dad's illness has been a blessing in disguise. Do you know what he told Dr. Shorter today?"

Stark shook his head and eased down onto the edge of the reception desk, bringing himself eye level with Meredith. "What did he tell her?"

"He told her that after our mom died, he started praying for God to make a way to bring us all home, to bring us all together again." She wiped tears from her eyes. "And here we are. Mom always preached that we kids had to be free to do our own thing, and she was right, but I'm not sure any of us saw that we could do that here. Until God showed us how. I'm so happy that you're my how, Stark Burns."

"Oh, but, Meri," he began, remembering that serious talk they were going to have.

Then she kissed him, and he was lost. The hands he meant to keep planted right there on the edge of the desk somehow wound up at her waist. He tried to take them away, but they began roaming her back, until one of them cupped her head. His arm locked her in place as the kiss deepened, and all he could think was that she belonged with him, was meant for him, not an alternate plan or a contingency plan but an *ultimate* plan.

The very idea seemed disloyal to Cathy and Bel, but he was helpless against his feelings for this woman. If anything should happen to her... But something already *had* happened to her, and if he wasn't careful he was going to make it worse. So much worse.

He pushed her back and jerked to the side in one frantic movement, gasping, "I am *so* sorry."

At first she looked stunned. Then a look of such consternation crossed her face that he thought she might hit him. Finally, she slumped down into the desk chair and rolled her eyes up at him, sighing.

"Right. Because I was stabbed."

Not wanting to loom over her, he went down on his haunches beside her. "You were more than stabbed."

"No," she said calmly, matter-of-factly, "I was stabbed. Period. It was the most harrowing, hurtful, traumatic experience of my life. Because of that one incident, I've been through counseling and self-defense training and spent a fortune on locks and cats. I learned to hate living in a big city, because that's where it happened, and I still have nightmares sometimes, mostly because my attacker was never caught, I think."

"Meri, I'm so sorry if I've contributed to that. I never meant—"

"Will you listen to me?" she interrupted sternly. "I'm going to tell you exactly what happened, and I want you to listen carefully. Then maybe you'll understand. All right?"

He wanted so much to take her hand, but he just nodded. "You don't have to tell me anything you don't want to."

"I want to tell you *everything*," she insisted. Getting up, she took him by the upper arms, made him rise and parked him on the edge of the desk again. Then she sat once more and began.

"At shift change, nearly all the nurses leave the hospital at the same time through the same door. I was late leaving that night. It just happened that I left the building by myself. I was walking to my car when this man jumped out from between two SUVs, grabbed me, held a knife to my throat and told me if I screamed or fought, he'd kill me."

Stark balled his hands into fists, wanting desperately to hit something, but that wouldn't help Meredith at all, so he forced himself to relax again. "Go on."

"He threw me down on the ground between the vehicles and started tearing at my clothes. He said that if I cooperated, let him do what he wanted, he wouldn't hurt me. But he'd already hurt me. I'd taken a hard knock on the back of my head and could tell that it was bleeding. And he'd done nothing to keep me from clearly seeing his face, so I didn't believe that he would leave me alive when he was done. Then I heard the door open again, and more than one person came out. I could hear them talking, so I knew *they* could hear *me*. I started screaming and fighting like crazy. When he couldn't quickly contain or quiet me, he stabbed me."

Stark shuddered, reminding himself aloud, "Your necklace deflected the blade."

"Yes, or it would have been much worse. The people heard and immediately ran to help me. He took off, literally stepped on me to get away. We were in a hospital staff parking lot, so medical help was right there."

Stark let that all sink in. She hadn't been raped. She'd been viciously attacked, terrified, traumatized, but not—Thank God!—raped. He was so glad for her. And he still wanted to get his hands on the man who had hurt her.

"You saw him. Why couldn't they catch him?"

She shrugged and shook her head. "The likeness they put together didn't match anything in their database, and he didn't leave a shred of DNA. He was cleanly shaved, even his head, and he wore long sleeves, gloves and a turtleneck."

Stark considered all the possible scenarios of that situation, horrified anew. "You were right to fight. He meant to kill you."

"I know he did. The police believed it was a crime of opportunity. I was the one woman who walked out that door alone that night. But for a full year, I had a hard time even leaving my apartment."

"But you did," Stark surmised, marveling at her courage.

"After about three weeks, I had to work and do other things," she said. "I didn't have to socialize, though. So I stayed home with my cats and pretended that was enough."

Stark shook his head. "You're still far braver than I am, Meri. I'm just now learning to face the world."

She got up out of her chair and stood next to him. "It's a different kind of trauma, Stark, a different kind of loss and pain."

He supposed that was true. "Still…"

"The point is," she said, "I've been over and over this in my head, and I've prayed and prayed about it. I'm not afraid. You can't use me as an excuse. If you want to push me out of your life, I can't stop you, but it's all on you."

He stared at her for a long moment, drinking in the beautiful honesty of her, trying to give it back to her. "I don't want to, Meri," he finally admitted. "I'm just so messed up."

"I know."

Her honesty allowed him to at last be honest with himself about his own motivations. He didn't like what he had to say, but she deserved the very best he could give her, however painful.

"The truth is, Meri, I'm not sure I can ever be what you need me to be, what you have a right to expect of any man. What I was for Cathy and Bel, I'm not sure I can be that again."

"Look how far you've come," she said, slipping her hands into the hair at the back of his head. "I think you're worth the risk."

"Aw, Meri." He couldn't agree and shook his head. "I want to be. Believe that at least."

Smiling, she kissed him again, and as he held her, he wondered if anything in the world could be as sweet as Meri's kiss. He didn't doubt for a moment that he loved her, and he knew now that he'd try to be what she needed simply because that was what she wanted, but...

No more excuses. No more looking for a way out.

That's what he'd been doing; he saw it now,

but from now on he would give it all he had, for Meri's sake. And pray it was enough.

Firmly in control, she broke the kiss after a moment and said, "Enough of that. We have work to do."

He smiled. Thankfully, at least one of them had some sense.

"I'm kitted up and ready to go," he told her. "It's going to be a busy afternoon, so I probably won't see you again today. If not, I'll see you in the morning. Call if you need me."

"Ditto."

He went to kiss her on the cheek, but she turned her head for a full-on lip-to-lip that made his heart swell.

"For the record," he told her softly, "I just don't want to hurt you."

"Thank you for that," she whispered, "and like I said, I think you're worth the risk."

"I hope you're right."

He prayed that she was right. Driving to and from every farm and ranch that day, every pasture, corral, pigsty, barn and rabbit hutch, he prayed that he wouldn't disappoint her.

Recalling what she'd said about being angry at God over her father's diagnosis, he thought back to something the pastor had preached on Sunday. The pastor had stated that God can take our anger, doubt and anything else we can dish out and is always waiting patiently for us to come back to Him. Maybe he was ready to go back to God, to start trusting again, to start believing again. Maybe that was part of trying again, of being who and what Meri needed and deserved.

Meri knew an excuse when she heard one. She should. She'd given herself plenty of excuses not to do what needed doing since the attack, most of which her trauma counselor had calmly, patiently knocked down. Stark needed and deserved someone to do that for him, too, but who had ever had the opportunity? Besides her?

Stark had loved his wife and daughter with a rare intensity, and Meredith loved him all the more for it. A man capable of that depth of feeling was a man worth fighting for, but Stark was also a man of uncommon strength, though he didn't seem to realize it. Only a very strong man could have survived such grief and put together any sort of functioning life all alone afterward.

If only he didn't blame himself for the accident, he might stop doubting that they could build a life together. If he could just face the memories of his past with some joy instead of grief, he might be able to think clearly about the accident and his part in it. Over that Monday afternoon, she racked her brain for ways to help him do that.

Something her counselor had said to her came to mind, something that Meredith herself had rejected at the time.

A supportive family can be a great catalyst. A family member who mirrors our feelings can confirm the rightness of our emotions or demonstrate their destructiveness. One who chooses a different path can challenge us to more fully investigate our emotional responses.

The counselor, provided by the hospital, had encouraged her to exclude her family from her treatment only if they were unsupportive, but Meredith had elected to keep them in the dark. She'd done it partly because she hadn't wanted to worry them, but also because her siblings wouldn't have been available to attend sessions with her anyway. If her mom had been alive, she wouldn't have hesitated to bring it up with her parents, but asking her dad to attend those counseling sessions alone with her had seemed awkward and unkind.

Stark had apparently never received any sort of counseling, but his family seemed quite supportive. An idea blossomed. She knew that she ought to ask Stark about it, but she also knew what he'd say. Did she dare ask him beforehand? She had the feeling that if she set the wheels in motion and then simply presented it to him as a done deal he might not be too happy but he'd go along. Still, it was a risk.

Half-a-dozen times she reached for the phone, intending either to discuss it with him or just put her plan into motion, but she held off. Each time, she prayed about it instead. At the end of the day, she considered hanging around, maybe making dinner for Stark. He obviously thought they should be more circumspect, though, and she very much respected that, so she locked up and went home.

Once there, however, she couldn't stop thinking about how to help him, so after dinner she kept the family at the table and put it to them.

"I want to invite Stark's family for Thanksgiving. I know it's last minute, Callie, but I'll do everything I can to help out. I—I just think he needs this, and Mr. Burns has told me point-blank that it would mean the world to them to spend the holiday with him."

"It's fine with me," Callie said, "but why doesn't he go there?"

Meredith blushed even as she smiled. "Frankly, we want to spend the holiday together."

Wes grinned at that, and Rex insincerely drawled, "No. Really?" He jumped when Callie jabbed him in the ribs with her elbow. "What I mean to say, baby sister, is that I'm glad you got over your Stark-anathema. He's really a great guy."

"He is," she said, "but it's not just that we want to be together this Thanksgiving and I want to be here." She told them what had happened to Stark's wife and daughter. She'd promised she wouldn't, but he was practically part of the family now. Surely he would understand.

"I knew there was something," Rex said, looking at Callie.

"Losing a spouse can be tough to deal with," she said softly. "To lose a spouse *and* a child…" She shook her head. "I don't even want to think about how it would have been for me without Bodie."

"Because of that, Stark finds it difficult to be around his sisters' families," Meri explained. "I guess they have daughters the same age as his and they spent a lot of time together or something. I just know that going there wouldn't be easy for him, so I thought if they came here, maybe..."

"A whole new frame of reference," Callie said. "Yeah, I can see that."

"Would you like me to make the call?" Wes asked.

Delighted, Meredith beamed. "We could do it together by speakerphone."

"Housing could be an issue," Callie murmured, "but Dad's got room at his place, and Ann and Dean could put up at least a couple of people. Bo can bunk with us."

"I don't mind sleeping on the couch," Meri volunteered.

"We'll make it work."

They didn't have to worry about providing beds. When Meredith and Wes spoke to Marvin Burns, he quickly conferred with his wife and accepted for the two of them and their younger son, Wayne, saying that "the girls" would spend the holiday with their grandparents. He also informed them that he and Mrs. Burns had purchased a motor home a few months ago and required only space to park it.

"We've got plenty of space at Straight Arrow," Wes assured them, "and any electrical hookups you might need, as well."

"This will be a real vacation for us," Marvin Burns enthused. "I can't tell you how excited we are. May I ask one question? Does Stark know we're coming?"

"Not yet," Meredith admitted. "I thought it best to, ah, clear it with everyone else before I proposed it to him."

"Might I suggest that we surprise him?" Marvin said.

Rex and Callie looked at each other and nodded. Callie said, "Oh, that would be fun."

Rex said, "We sure owe Stark for all he's done around here."

"Your son's quite the vet," Wes put in. "I doubt one in a hundred doctors could've saved my old horse Soldier earlier this fall."

"That's some compliment," Marvin said. "We're in agreement, then."

Meri had her doubts about this, but with everyone else going along, she hated to be the naysayer in the group, especially as this had been her idea. Besides, what argument could she offer against surprising Stark without making him seem unreasonable?

"Meredith," Marvin said, "I cannot thank you enough. I knew the first time I heard your voice that you were the answer to our prayers."

She hoped that was true. Oh, how she hoped that was true.

"I look forward to meeting you all in person, sir."

"Not half as much as we look forward to meeting all of you and seeing our son again," he said.

Mrs. Burns got on then, her excitement palpable. She and Callie talked menu, and she said she'd bring a sweet-potato casserole and buttermilk-pecan pie, both of which were favorites of Stark's from his boyhood. Finally, Wes and Marvin spoke of addresses and directions before they ended the call.

"Something tells me this is going to be a Thanksgiving to remember," Rex said, getting up from the table.

"I'll say," Wes agreed. "Callie's dad will be here and Dean's grandma. And just think about how much we have to be thankful for."

"Boggles the mind," Callie said, rising to take her daughter from her high chair. It was not an easy process.

"Bodie's just about outgrown that chair," Wes noted, taking his granddaughter onto his lap. Callie shared a secretive smile with her husband, and sudden insight hit Meri with the impact of a hammer blow.

"Oh, my word, you're pregnant!" she blurted.

Callie gaped at her, but Rex beamed. "How did you know?" Callie asked.

"The way you looked at Rex just now."

Wes whooped, startling Bodie into grabbing him around the neck.

"Papa yell!" she scolded, shaking a little finger at him.

"Sorry, honey, I'm just so pleased," he told her. Hugging her, he glanced around, his blue eyes sparkling. "There's one more for the Thanksgiving list!"

"At least you won't have to cook for this one. Yet," Rex teased his wife, wrapping his arms around Callie from behind.

"We just confirmed it and were saving the news for a Thanksgiving surprise," Callie explained, "but seeing as we have a surprise anyway, I don't suppose it matters."

"If I'd known you were expecting, though, I wouldn't even have suggested—" Meri began.

Callie waved that away. "No, it's okay. I feel fine. Not a bit of morning sickness or anything."

"Still, I'll help every way I can."

"You would've anyway. I'm much more concerned about how my father is going to take this news now that he's accepted me into his business."

"He knows you can handle any business

concerns, motherhood, a household and anything else that comes your way," Rex told her.

"You mean that *we* can handle anything that comes *our* way. You're the son-in-law he always wanted now, you know."

Rex chuckled. "True. Besides, he's a long way from retirement."

Meri got up and went around the table to hug her brother and sister-in-law. "I'm so happy for the two of you."

"I'm happy for you," Callie told her. "Stark is a good man."

"Let's don't get the cart before the horse," Meri cautioned. "Things are a long way from being settled between us."

"I haven't seen Stark Burns in church with anyone else," Wes pointed out.

That was true, but they knew so little about Stark's grief and guilt, about the depth and duration of his separation from his parents and family, about the shallowness and barrenness of his life.

What if Stark never wanted to have another child? She didn't think she could live without that.

What if he truly couldn't bear to see his parents and brother on Thanksgiving again?

What if he never forgave her for inviting them here?

What if he simply did not care enough for her to put the past behind him?

She trembled inwardly with fear even as she smiled in celebration of her brother's joy.

Chapter Twelve

For most folks the week before Thanksgiving tended to be slow businesswise. They traveled or turned their minds to things other than commerce, but Stark didn't travel and hadn't expected to have anything on his mind other than business, so he'd agreed to board some local pets. Add to that a sick milk cow, a dog hit by a car, another that ate an entire package of chocolate bars, a gerbil that got into cleanser, and a stupid rooster and a cat that would not stop tearing up each other, and the two days remaining before Thanksgiving were anything but tranquil. He and Meri seemed to be running every minute of the day, and the place was rarely quiet.

Young Hardy Wilson's basset hound pup had howled from the moment it had been dropped off. The only time during the day that the pup was quiet was when it was draped over Meri's lap. Unfortunately, with everything else going on, she couldn't sit with the thing constantly, and when that pup howled, the Perkinsons' blind old poodle barked. Shrilly. Even Louise Shepherd's near-deaf bulldog could hear it, and he sounded like a foghorn when he joined in. Stark hadn't seen his cat since the basset hound had arrived, and the only way to get any sleep at night was to take the pup into his bed, which was apparently what Hardy had been doing.

Meredith had told him about Rex and Callie's pregnancy, which had rocked him, though he'd tried not to show it. When the time came, he'd be happy for them. Surely by then he could be happy for them. He wasn't that selfish and self-involved that he couldn't be happy for a friend. They already had one daughter, and everything was fine. So far.

He remembered the happy, warm, exhausting, joy-filled days of early fatherhood. And the endless, hollow, cold, sleepless, grief-stricken years of loss following the death of his daughter.

Maybe if he and Cathy had had a surviving child he'd have managed better, found more reason to pull himself together and go on. He hoped so. He wanted to believe that was true.

He chose to believe that was true. But the idea of bringing another innocent child into the world to suffer and die troubled him on a level that he couldn't quite look at yet. With time and Meri's help, maybe... He couldn't face the possibility, and why should he? They were a long way from that. Weren't they?

By Thursday, Stark was more than ready to escape what felt increasingly like bedlam. Meredith had told him they'd eat around lunchtime, but that he should come on over as early as he liked. He didn't pretend, even to himself, that he wasn't looking forward to the day, so as soon as he'd taken care of his boarders, he cleaned up and headed over to the Straight Arrow, keeping breakfast to coffee and an overripe banana.

The day had turned out surprisingly warm and bright. When he stepped up onto the front porch of the ranch house, Meri came out the front door wearing an apron over her jeans. She'd rolled up the long sleeves of her pink-and-blue plaid shirt and secured her hair with a clip atop her head in a messy pile that was altogether fetching. On her feet were sensible athletic shoes, and she hadn't applied a speck of makeup. Just the sight of her made him happy and loosened his tongue.

"You are the most gorgeous woman I've ever seen."

He declared it without even thinking, without any sort of filter or consideration for who might be listening or watching. She laughed, but the sound had a nervous edge to it, and he regretted his impulsiveness at once.

Had he been this impulsive and uncontrolled with Cathy? No, he hadn't. He'd been self-assured and calm, completely certain of his path and his welcome, as well as the outcome. He'd never had a moment of doubt, and if Cathy had, she'd never let on.

Meri twisted her hands in her apron, saying, "Stark, I have to tell you something."

Stepping up onto the porch, he took her hands in his. "What is it, babe?"

Taking a deep breath, she began, "I, uh, I…" She grimaced and then spoke quickly. "I told my family about the accident."

Somehow, he was neither surprised nor upset. "You told them what happened to Cathy and Bel."

"Yes. I know I promised not to, but—"

"It had to happen sometime," he reasoned.

She looked up sharply. "You don't mind?"

Smiling, he lightly grasped her chin between his thumb and forefinger, then positioned her head so he wouldn't have to remove his hat and kissed her. She was what mattered now. He was working hard to show her that, and it must have been getting through, because she wrapped her arms around him.

The screen door creaked, but Meri didn't pull back. Pleased, Stark didn't either. Statement time, then. That was all right by him. It seemed to be Declaration Day.

Dean's voice said, "Okay, you two. Break it up and get in here. There's about to be a big announcement. Or should I say, *another* big announcement?"

Grinning, Stark broke the kiss and lifted his head. "Is this about the baby?"

Dean looked stunned, poleaxed. "How did you know?"

Meri turned within the curve of Stark's arm. "I figured it out Monday night."

His brows drawing together, Dean echoed, "Monday night?"

She nodded. "Callie confirmed it for the rest of us Monday night."

Clearly flummoxed, Dean threw up his hands. "How did Callie know?"

Meredith mirrored his gesture, throwing up her own hands. "Well, she's the one who's pregnant. Duh."

Stark thought Dean's eyes might fall out of his head before he abruptly turned, yanked open the door and bolted inside, yelling, "Ann! Callie's pregnant, too!"

Too? Meri turned a shocked face on Stark, then ran for the door.

He stood rooted where she'd left him. Two pregnancies. Whoa. That was a lot to take in.

A second later, Meri burst through the door again, grabbed him by the hand and tugged him inside. Pure habit made him pluck off his hat. He tried for a peg on the foyer wall but missed it and so had his hat in his hand when they reached the living room. Callie and Ann—the former garbed in an apron, a wooden spoon in hand—were hugging and babbling about due dates and symptoms with an older woman whom Stark took to be Dean's grandmother, while Wes cackled like a laying hen and Rex and Dean jabbed at each other verbally.

"Didn't waste any time, farm boy," Rex was saying.

"What'd you expect? I'm a young go-getter," Dean retorted, playing on the fact that he was a few years younger than his wife. "You can't afford to waste any time, old man."

Old man? That stung. At thirty-seven, Rex was actually three years *younger* than Stark, who suddenly felt ancient. Meri, on the other hand, was only twenty-six. Of course she would want babies. Lots of babies. He watched her hug her sister and sister-in-law, laughing and congratulating them. Then she hugged her brother and brother-in-law and finally her dad, while Stark stood there, feeling like an interloper—until she came and slipped her arm about his waist. With that one simple gesture, he somehow belonged, if only on the edges of it all.

"Wow. This place is going to be a madhouse next year," she said, laughing.

Wes came over and wrapped his arm around her shoulders so that he and Stark bracketed her. "If only your mother were here," he said.

Meri nodded. "I know. I miss her, too."

"You, more than any of the others, I think," Wes said, dropping a kiss onto the top of her head. "You're so like her, the spitting image of her. She was the making of me, that woman. Didn't know how I'd go on after she died, with all you kids gone. Now look at us. Life is good again. Life is *good* again. So much to be thankful for." He reached over and clapped Stark on the shoulder. "Glad you're here, son."

Suddenly, Stark could smile again, relax. He put aside his doubts and wrapped an arm around Meri's shoulders while Wes went to answer Donovan's questions. At "almost six," as he made sure everyone knew, the boy wasn't quite clear on what all these babies meant.

"You're getting one baby. Either a brother or a sister. Bodie's also getting a baby brother or sister. Her baby brother or sister will be your cousin, and your baby brother or sister will be her cousin."

"Unless somebody has twins," Meri put in.

Both Ann and Callie glared at her and scolded, "Bite your tongue!"

Dean's grandmother laughed and winked at Wes. "We'd be okay with twins, wouldn't we, Grandpa?"

"Oh, yeah. Or triplets."

Callie and Ann both howled, while the two elders laughed. Stark bent low enough to speak into Meri's ear. "That's Dean's grandmother, right?"

"Oh, I'm so sorry," she said. "In all the confusion, I forgot." She dragged him over to introduce him.

"It's a pleasure to meet you, Mrs. Pryor."

"Oh, it's just Betty," she said, "or Grandma, if you like. Everyone else calls me Grandma."

"You're not old enough to be my grandma," he told her. "Betty will do. So, of course, I'm Stark."

Just then a loud hiss sounded from the

kitchen. Callie yelped and ran in that direction, with Ann following her through the dining room.

"Pleased to meet you, Stark," Betty called, hurrying after them.

Meri popped up onto her toes to kiss Stark's chin, saying, "I'll bring you something to drink when I get a chance." Then she headed off after them. "What do you prefer? Coffee or iced tea?"

"Coffee," he called as she pushed through the swinging door into the kitchen.

All at once it was just men and kids in the living room. Wes kicked back in his recliner, parked Bodie in his lap, picked up the remote control and pointed it at the flat-screen TV.

"Gentlemen," he announced, "it's football time."

Stark hadn't watched football since… He cut off the thought. This was a day for new beginnings. He hung up his hat, returning to sit on the end of the couch. It quickly became obvious that Rex and Dean chose opposite sides just to have a reason to bicker. If Wes had a preference, he wasn't saying so. Thankfully, no one asked Stark, but he couldn't help commenting from time to time. Whenever he did, everyone looked at him oddly.

Meri came into the room with his coffee as Wes asked, "Did you play?"

"Just through high school."

"You know a lot about the game."

"His dad is a coach," she said.

"Really. What team?" Dean asked.

"It's a private school," Stark answered.

Rex, who had lived in Tulsa, put it together. "Wow. Coach Burns is revered in Tulsa."

Stark nodded, noticing that Rex and Wes traded looks. Callie poked her head through the kitchen door just then, and announced, "Uh, dinner's going to be a little late, guys. Anyone want an appetizer?"

Assuming that something had boiled over or burned during the baby celebration, Stark shrugged. The others jumped on the appetizer bandwagon, however, and soon he was chowing down on chips and dip. That quickly played out, however. Meri ran upstairs, saying she wanted to comb her hair and put on a little makeup.

For some reason she seemed nervous when she came back down, perching on the arm of the sofa next to him, her arm around his shoulders. She'd changed into a filmy pink blouse over a matching tank top, replacing her athletic shoes with flirty little flats. She kept glancing at the clock on the mantel. Rex and Wes were doing the same thing. Stark began to get the feeling that he was missing something. Then he heard a vehicle and realized everyone had been waiting for a late arrival.

That's when things really got strange. Meri glanced at him guiltily before hopping up and running to the door. Everybody in the room came to their feet, so naturally Stark followed suit. Then the women all poured in from the kitchen. He heard Meri out on the porch talking to someone.

That almost sounded like... Was that his *mother*? He heard something about a late start and someone who refused to be left behind.

The next thing he knew, Meri stood at his side again, her arm around his waist, her anxious face turned up to his. Her pretty lips silently formed the words *please... Please*.

Confused, he glanced around, but everyone else's attention was on the foyer, so that's where he looked next. And saw his parents. His mom and dad. There. With Meri and her family. And him. Shocked, he felt Meredith's arm tighten about his waist and looked down once more. He knew instantly that she expected him to be angry because she'd arranged this, but somehow it all felt so *right*.

He could only shake his head, chuckling.

All he could think to say was, "You warned me." She'd told him that she would push until he stopped her. In that moment, he felt nothing but gladness.

He smiled at his parents—and saw his brother, Wayne, behind them. That gave him pause. If Wayne was here, too, could his sisters and their families be far behind? He swallowed down the rising panic. He didn't want to ruin this day. Somehow he had to push forward.

He shook his head and said, "Mom, Dad, it's good to see you. Wayne, you, too."

Everyone seemed to relax. His parents started forward, and so did he. His mom said, "It's good to see you, too, son, so good. Your sisters send their love. They're spending the holiday with your grandparents. We couldn't leave them all alone."

Relieved, Stark swept Meredith along with him. Then when he reached his parents, he enveloped them both in his arms. "What a day for surprises."

He turned to Wes, glanced at Rex, once more gathered Meri against him, and said, "Thank y'all so much."

Meri started making introductions. Smiling, Stark placed his hands on her shoulders, thinking that this was, indeed, a day for new beginnings. That's when Wayne stepped to one side, and it all fell apart.

A small tornado with long black hair and blue eyes shoved her way through the adults clustered together and threw herself at him, bellowing, "Uncle Stark!"

Horrified, he stared down into the achingly familiar little face, tears instantly filling his eyes. "Belinda."

Suddenly, he was back there again, looking down into that little pink coffin, his heart shattering, the old agony ripping through him.

Don't drop me, Daddy! Don't drop me!

Hold still then, Belindaworm.

Wake up, Bel. Please wake up.

"No, Uncle Stark! It's Jeanie Ruth."

Six-and-a-half-year-old Jeanie Ruth, who was so determined to be loved. By everyone. Even the uncle who had done his best to avoid her from the day of his daughter's funeral. Jeanie Ruth, his sister Sarah's daughter, who was the very image of his own sweet Bel. They could have been twins born three years and three months apart, but were opposite sides of the same coin in every other way. Belinda had been sweet, passive and shy, while Jeanie Ruth was strong willed, unusually prescient and canny in an adorable little-girl way that made one wonder if she wouldn't grow up to rule the world. She certainly seemed determined to rule everyone around her, especially the uncle who did his best to keep his contact with her to a minimum.

Small for her age, but big on leverage of any sort, Jeanie Ruth had soaked up all the family talk about her resemblance to Belinda, and to her that meant Uncle Stark should grovel at her feet. She didn't understand the pain that even talk or memories of Bel brought him. She only knew that he should adore her. He did love her. He just couldn't bear to be around her.

What could he do in that moment but what he'd always done? He endured her hug, patting her little back impassively, and locked away the urge to run, along with every other emotion. Within moments he felt the familiar, safe old numbness steal over him.

Meredith introduced Jeanie Ruth to Donovan and then to Bodie. A toy box had been brought down to the mudroom for the little ones, and Jeanie Ruth immediately took charge of the play. Meredith went so far as to bring down her cat, banishing Donovan's beloved dog to the outdoors.

A little while later, Stark sat in a corner of the couch, staring at the television while the others chatted companionably around him and the children played in the other room. He couldn't help wondering how soon he could politely leave. Wayne kept trying to talk to him, but Stark continually interrupted with comments about the game until Wayne simply went away. His father asked him a question about his practice, and he had to filter through what he could remember of the conversation around him before he could formulate a reply.

"It's fine."

"It seems that Meredith has been a big help to you."

"Yes." Stark purposefully narrowed his field of vision to the TV so he wouldn't have to see her reaction. It was a trick he'd learned long ago. "She helped streamline things. Got it all organized. I can probably handle it on my own again now."

If that caused any shock or consternation, he didn't see it, didn't want to see it. His attention was fixed firmly on the game. He would probably never watch another football game, so he might as well enjoy this one, though he couldn't really have said that he was enjoying anything about this day.

He knew for certain now. He knew that he simply was not capable of what Meredith would ask of him. She had done her best for him, and he appreciated her efforts. At the very least, she had made his life more comfortable. He would always thank her for that, but it couldn't be anything else. He simply didn't have anything else in him.

What Meri wanted from him, what she deserved to have, had died that October afternoon four years ago with Cathy and Bel. He'd been fooling himself, trying to believe he could have it all again.

Today he would be thankful for what he'd had and ask for nothing more than peace. He just wanted peace.

Couldn't God give him just that much?

He wouldn't think of Jeanie Ruth and her grasping little arms, her need for an uncle's love. She had others to love her, so many others.

He wouldn't think of Meredith or her trauma. She was brave and whole and unspeakably beautiful, too wonderful for a wreck of a man like him. Some other man would claim her, a whole man, a more deserving man.

He wouldn't think of that man, a better man than him.

He wouldn't even think of his parents. They had another son and daughters, grandchildren who lived and played and loved. They didn't need the constant shadow of his grief throwing a pall over every family gathering.

He wouldn't think at all. Or feel. Or want. He would just breathe.

How long, Lord, he wondered silently, *do I have to breathe and pretend to like it?*

Somehow he got through dinner. There were not enough chairs or room at either table, so he made sure he was last in line and ate sitting on the sofa. Meri insisted on joining him.

He knew he'd be sick if he had to eat dessert, so he let Callie package it for him to take home, which he did as soon as possible, despite the complaints. After all, he had a ready-made excuse.

"I have to see to the animals in the kennel."

"On Thanksgiving?" his mother protested.

"If I'd known you were coming, I wouldn't have agreed to board them," he said, returning her hug.

"That is my fault," his father confessed. "I wanted to surprise you."

Stark knew the truth. His parents had feared he'd find a way to keep them from coming if he'd known beforehand. They were likely correct, especially if he'd known Jeanie Ruth would be with them.

"We'll see you tomorrow, won't we?" his

mother asked. "We don't have to leave before evening."

"You don't have any appointments," Meredith pointed out hopefully.

He tried for a reassuring smile. "Barring any emergencies. But, of course, there is the kennel."

"We'd like to see your place," his father suggested.

"Nothing much to see," Stark hedged.

"I could bring them by after breakfast," Meredith offered.

One more day, he thought, not answering. Surely he could survive one more day. And then what?

He couldn't pick up with Meredith as if nothing had happened. She had told him that she would push until he stopped her. Well, the time had come to put a stop to this lunacy, for both their sakes. This needed to be handled and handled now. He was man enough, at least, to do this.

"Meredith," he asked, "will you walk me out?"

She must have sensed it coming, because for once she didn't brighten. She simply nodded.

He tried to feel relief.

He tried to feel rightness, because this was surely the best thing to do.

He tried to feel regret.

Something.

All he felt was *sadness*, the great, overwhelming sadness that had been his life for four long years now. *Before* Meri.

The sadness that would *always* be his life.

Chapter Thirteen

The moment Meri had seen Stark's reaction to his niece, she knew she had blundered badly. Of course, she hadn't known that Jeanie Ruth would accompany Marvin and Andi Burns. Apparently, even they hadn't expected to bring the strong-willed child with them, but, according to Wayne, she had thrown such a fit that morning that the family had feared she would ruin Thanksgiving for her frail great-grandparents if left behind. With time escaping, they'd finally agreed to bring her just to get on the road.

Still, Meri knew that she should have foreseen catastrophe. Hadn't she felt uneasy about this whole surprise thing from the beginning? Why hadn't she insisted on telling Stark what they'd planned?

The answer to that question was simple.

She hadn't told him because she'd feared he would be angry and refuse to take part. At the heart of it, she'd feared he would be angry with *her*. It had been her idea to invite his parents here for Thanksgiving, after all.

Even though she didn't understand exactly what had gone wrong, she knew that she'd ruined the day for Stark, and she could only apologize for that. Before launching into it, she made sure to pull the front door closed behind them when they stepped out onto the porch.

"I am so, so sorry. I should have told you they were coming." When he would have spoken, she held up a hand. "Let me rephrase that. I should have asked you before we invited them."

He crammed his hat onto his head, not looking at her, and said, "You were just trying to make everyone happy. That's what you do."

She didn't quite know how to take that. It sounded hopeful, but he still hadn't looked at her. "I thought it would h-help."

"You didn't know Jeanie Ruth would be with them," he said after a moment ripe with tension, "or that she looks enough like my daughter to be her twin."

Meredith caught her breath. "Oh, Stark." She reached out a comforting hand, but he shifted away from her. A chill swept over her, a bitter cold that had nothing to do with the pleasant, surprisingly still afternoon.

"It's like seeing Bel come back from…" He let that go, swallowing, and squared his shoulders. "You'd think I'd get over it." He shook his head. "But I don't. And I'm not going to, Meredith. That's the thing I have to face. The thing we both have to face." He looked at her finally, his dark eyes filled with such sadness that she clapped a hand over her mouth to keep from crying out. "I can't. I'm sorry, but I just can't."

She knew what he was saying. He didn't have to spell it out. "Stark," she began, instinctively reaching out to him again. He stepped back. "Listen to me. One day, I know, you'll want to be a father again. You'll realize—"

"If you knew, really knew, you wouldn't ask that of me."

The calmness of his words terrified her.

"All right," she said, aware that her voice trembled. "That doesn't mean—"

"It means," he interrupted gently, "that I can't see you anymore."

"No, Stark. Don't say that. Please. Just think for a minute."

"Don't come back to work," he told her, his voice deep and even.

"No. Stark. No. Please." But he had already stepped off the porch and was walking down the path away from her. "Stark," she whispered, clinging to the upright post so she wouldn't collapse into a blubbering heap. She wanted to shout, but that would only alert those in the house, and if she had any hope of changing his mind...if she had any hope...

She stood there for—she didn't know how long—too stunned to move, let alone weep or even pray. Something cold and clammy touched the inside of her wrist, making her jump. Glancing down, she found Donovan's aggravating dog, Digger, staring up at her.

"Stop that!" she commanded, rubbing the spot where it had touched her with its nose. The dog tilted its head and rose up on its hind legs, leaning against her with its forepaws. A claw snagged in the delicate fabric of her overblouse. "Down!"

Just as the dog plopped back to all fours, the front door opened, and Donovan and Jeanie Ruth ran out.

"Aunt Meri!" Donovan cried happily. "Me and Jeanie Ruth is going to sleep over!"

"That's fine," Meredith said grudgingly, tugging on her blouse and glaring at the dog, "as long as that beast of yours stays at your house."

"But Digger always stays with me," Donovan said, obviously dismayed.

"He ruined my blouse!" Meredith snapped. "And he terrorizes my cat."

"He don't terrorsize our cats."

"I want that animal kept at your place!" Meredith insisted.

"I want to sleep over at your house anyhow," Jeanie Ruth said, folding her arms. "I want to play in your tree house."

"But Granny Andi said we had to sleep here. We can play at my house tomorrow," Donovan pointed out.

"What about your dog?" Jeanie Ruth asked slyly.

Donovan went down on his knees, petting the dog. "I'll see you tomorrow, boy."

Meredith turned to see Ann standing in the doorway, a frown on her face. "The cat's going to be in your room anyway, isn't it, Meri?"

"If someone doesn't let it out," Meredith muttered, pushing past her into the foyer.

Dean and her father stood there. Dean said, "The dog is trained to protect Donovan because he goes to the fields with me so often."

So what does he need protection from

here? Meri wondered, heading for the stairs. What in this house could possibly harm him? Broken hearts weren't contagious, after all.

As she started up the stairs, her father said, "We have company, Meredith."

"I have a headache." Only as she said it did she realize that it was so. Her head pounded with every beat of her aching heart.

She heard Callie say, "You must've eaten something that disagreed with you. I'll bring you something for it."

Falling onto her bed, Meredith felt the cat hop up next to her and cradled it close, even as the throbbing in her skull blinded her. Callie roused her moments later. She swallowed pills with water, gasping with the pain in her head, but though the pain receded, true sleep did not come. Instead, unwelcome thoughts crept in.

Her whole world had fallen apart. She'd lost the man she loved and her job at the same time. She would have to return to Oklahoma City to work, after all. But what did it matter? She couldn't imagine making a life with any man other than Stark. Worst of all was thinking of Stark slipping back into the half-life that he'd been living. She hadn't helped him at all, hadn't truly improved his life one bit.

He didn't love her, didn't want her. He

didn't love anyone or anything but his grief. That meant he might as well have died with Cathy and Belinda, and *that* truly broke her heart.

Finally the tears came. She tried to pray, but the words wouldn't form. All she could think was, *Please, please, please...*

At some point, she realized that the house had quieted. Then, in the silence that should have meant the household was sleeping, she heard something that sounded very much like the front door opening. Troubled, Meredith sat up in bed.

She hadn't undressed, but she had kicked off her shoes. Barefoot, she stood and padded to the door of her bedroom. She opened it a crack, hearing more creaks and groans. The cat tried to slip out, so she bent and picked it up. Cradling Tiger against her, she stepped out into the hall and heard giggling voices downstairs. Obviously, the kids were up and about instead of sleeping.

Intending to put them back to bed, she padded silently down the stairs and into the living room, where a pair of pallets had been laid. One of them had been abandoned, and a light shined from beneath a blanket tented over the other. She hadn't taken two full steps in that direction before a raucous barking started.

Tiger screeched and leaped out of her arms. He bounced off the lamp next to her dad's recliner—which Meri managed to catch before it hit the floor—skidded a U-turn and raced back up the stairs, the dog after it, trailing a blanket and other bedding.

"Digger!" Donovan shouted, halting the dog in its tracks.

Meredith got the lamp righted and the light on about the time that her father showed up, wearing his undershirt and jeans.

"What's going on?"

She glared at the two little miscreants kneeling on the pallet, Jeanie Ruth clutching a flashlight, Donovan holding on to the dog that had slunk back to him.

"I'll tell you what's going on," Meredith said harshly. "They were sneaking the dog into the house." She shook a finger at Donovan. "And after I told you to keep that nasty canine away from here!" She went over and opened the door, ordering, "Digger. Out!"

"Meredith," her father said as the dog trotted out the door.

"No, Dad." She closed the door behind the animal and locked it for good measure. "Digger chased my cat back up the stairs. Who knows where Tiger's hiding? Your lamp was almost broken." And her headache was back, full throttle. She squeezed her temples between her thumb and forefinger. "I'm going to bed."

She passed Rex and Callie on the stairs.

"Way to go, sis," Rex muttered.

"Leave her alone," Callie admonished softly. "She's not feeling well."

"She'd feel fine if Stark had stayed," Rex said.

Meri was blubbering by the time she got to her room. The stupid cat sat on the foot of her bed, grooming himself. She threw herself down beside Tiger and sobbed into her pillow. Did the whole family know that Stark had fired her and thrown her out of his life? If not, they would soon. Big surprise. Hadn't she always been the sister who didn't quite measure up?

The others had made big splashes in their chosen career fields. She had gotten herself stabbed and then hidden from everyone and everything but the most basic employment. They'd come home and found love, started families. She'd fallen for the one man who didn't, couldn't, want her and was destined to slink back to her lonely apartment with her stupid cat.

Maybe she was the crazy cat lady, after all.

Just before dawn she calmed enough to get

up and wash her face. Staring at her reflection in the mirror, she saw that she looked the way she felt—haggard, eyes and nose swollen and red, utterly bereft, but she knew that she'd been unreasonable and unkind to everyone around her, especially the kids. She owed them an apology, Donovan most of all.

She certainly wasn't going to sleep, so she might as well get a start on the morning. Callie had put up several pans of her famous sticky buns for breakfast this morning. Meredith could start them on their final rising and warm the oven. While she was waiting, she could use cold compresses on her eyes, try to look human before Stark's parents put in an appearance. She didn't know what she was going to say to them, how to handle this day. She'd just have to let it play out and trust God with the results.

What did she have to lose at this point? Her own handiwork had yielded nothing but disaster. She didn't know how much disaster until she tiptoed down the stairs, her athletic shoes in her hands—to find the front door open and the living room, along with both pallets, completely empty.

It must have been near dawn before Stark finally closed his eyes in sleep. He hadn't fully realized how indelibly Meredith had put her stamp on this place until he'd driven up yesterday afternoon and, from sheer habit, parked in the second carport. As he'd walked past the shower, he'd seen the first example of her handiwork. Cleaning up outside was much more pleasant now. No doubt, if he'd kept her on, she would have had that thing enclosed soon.

When he'd fitted his key into the lock on the door, he'd realized that he hadn't asked for Meri's keys back, but then he knew that he could never do that. It would be the same as saying that he didn't trust her with the drugs and medical paraphernalia around the clinic, and he did. Implicitly.

He'd walked through the back hall, hearing his boarders' din. He'd cared for them, crated the pup and hauled it along with him as he'd wandered the building, noting all the ways Meri had improved the place. Pity she hadn't managed it with him, but facts were facts, and he had learned the hard way that he had to face them.

His wife and daughter had been killed, and it was as much his fault as anyone's.

Except…was it really anyone's fault?

The insurance company had told his father that a restraining strap inside the trailer had broken, allowing the load to shift when the rig had taken the on-ramp. True, the driver may have been traveling a little faster than the recommended speed, but he'd probably taken that same ramp at that same speed in that same tractor-trailer rig dozens of times in the past with no problems. And while Stark had delayed their travel to watch the game, they'd left early in the fourth quarter when it had become apparent that one team was going to win handily. Besides, they'd driven into Tulsa on those same roads at those same times more often than he could even recall.

Accidents happened. But if accidents happened, then God allowed them, for reasons entirely His own, reasons we might not see or appreciate but were supposed to trust were somehow best.

That meant that God allowed death— which, according to Scripture, was exactly what humanity deserved, what humanity had chosen, the direct result of sin entering the world. It hurt. It *seemed* unfair, but wasn't. Because God had a plan. He always had a plan.

The fact was Stark loved Meredith Billings and his little niece Jeanie Ruth Camber.

Why couldn't he bear to be with either one of them? Why couldn't he find the courage to take what Meri offered? To look at Jeanie Ruth and remember his daughter with happiness, as well as grief? How did he join the living again?

He honestly didn't think he could. Without Meri.

A new grief had swamped him with that realization. He had faced life without Cathy and Bel. Now he must face life without them *and* without Meri. When the full impact of that had hit him, he'd fallen to his knees, crushed in body and spirit.

Eventually, exhausted by the emotional outburst, he'd tugged off his boots, tossed aside his shirt and collapsed onto the bed, searching through hours of empty darkness for the numbness that had protected him for so long. It had deserted him again, however, and every time he'd closed his eyes, he'd seen Meredith's shattered expression or Jeanie Ruth's determined one. When he could no longer ignore the pup's distress, he'd taken the little fellow out to relieve himself, returned him to his crate and fallen back into bed.

At last, sleep had come—and seemingly moments later someone pounded on his door, a man's voice calling his name. The cacophony that came with three strange dogs in the house immediately erupted. Blearily, Stark rolled to his feet, finding his wrinkled shirt.

"Coming!"

It must be a true emergency for someone to come pounding on his door with dawn a mere suggestion on the horizon. He slung on his shirt, jabbing his arms into the sleeves, as he padded barefoot to the front door. He flipped the dead bolt, yawning, and pulled open the door, feeling the sharp edge of a stiffening breeze.

"What's the problem?"

Wes Billings stood on his doorstep, his truck idling not four feet away, the driver's door standing open.

"The kids are gone."

"What?"

"Donovan and Jeanie Ruth, they're gone. Disappeared. Took off in the night, near as we can tell. Andi says the girl has a sort of fixation on you. We hoped they might have come here."

"No! I haven't seen them."

Wes rubbed a hand over the white fuzz atop his head. "It was a long shot, but no one else has seen them. If they'd walked to Dean and Ann's, they'd have been there by now, or we'd have passed them on the road."

"Who's looking?" Stark asked, hastily snapping closed his shirt.

"Everyone. Sheriff's put out an Amber Alert in case someone picked them up. I'm checking the diner next. Donovan was telling Jeanie Ruth all about it, so maybe they went there."

"That doesn't make sense."

"No, it doesn't, but we're grasping at straws here. If they didn't go to Dean's and they didn't go to the motorhome, and they didn't come to you, where else is there?"

"The school maybe?" Stark suggested, racking his sleepy brain.

"I'll check that, too." Wes shook his head. "If anything happens to those kids, Meredith won't be the only one going insane."

"Meredith?"

Sighing, Wes rubbed a finger over a thin eyebrow that hadn't been there two weeks ago. "Meredith wasn't herself last night. She was a little…harsh about the dog. She caught them sneaking it into the house after everyone went to bed. She threw out the dog, scolded Donovan." He shook his head. "She's blaming herself for this."

Shame, fear and determination filled Stark. He hung his head. "No, this isn't her fault. It's mine."

"Stark," Wes said, "this isn't about blame. This is about finding those kids."

Stark nodded. Finding those kids and fixing his many mistakes.

"I'll put on my boots and get out to the ranch."

"I'll call if I find anything," Wes said, turning back to his truck.

"Same," Stark promised, closing the door.

He yanked on his boots, ignoring the dogs. They weren't due for meals and exercise for hours yet, and it wouldn't hurt them if either were late. He'd get back to them as soon as possible. The most important thing at the moment was getting to Meri and finding those kids.

Grabbing his jacket and hat, he locked up and hit the road. On the way, he thought about what must have happened. Meredith must have banished the dog, which wouldn't have pleased Donovan. Jeanie Ruth, who was used to getting her way, must have convinced him to leave with the dog, but where would they have gone other than to the Pryor place?

Wes had said they should've been there by now or been found. If they'd taken the road. What if they *hadn't* taken the road? Donovan might have struck out across the fields and pastures for home, not realizing some of the obstacles and dangers that lay in the way.

The only real wildlife concern would be skunks, which were more often rabid than any other animal. Donovan would know to steer clear, but Jeanie Ruth might not, and she was nothing if not strong willed. When she made up her mind to do something, most adults couldn't derail her, let alone another child. Still, the last rabies warning Stark had received had been in late summer. It *should* be fine. If they were even out there.

But where else could they be?

He asked himself that question over and over again as he tore along that red dirt road to the ranch, which was massive, as he realized all too well. As he pulled to a stop, he saw that the motorhome in which his parents were apparently traveling was not there, so they must be out looking. Rex's truck was gone, along with Wes's, of course, and the pair of ATVs that were normally parked in the front of the barn. Meri's little coupe sat in its customary spot, however.

Stark's left foot hit the ground almost before the engine died, and he was jogging before the truck door slammed shut, leaving his hat behind for once. He loped along the path to the house, trying not to think about the chill in the wind, knocked, then simply opened the door and walked in. "Meri!" he called.

A sniffle told him where to find her. Two long strides carried him through the entry and into the living room. There he found something he'd never expected to see.

The woman he loved in the arms of his brother.

Chapter Fourteen

Wayne nodded grimly and dropped his arms, but Meredith didn't even lift her head, wiping her eyes and nose with a handkerchief, instead. He knew then what an absolute idiot he was, what a self-deluding, lying fool he could be.

As if he could let her go to another man, love another man. He'd beat bloody the next man who touched her. That included his own brother, and he glared at Wayne to let him know that.

Wayne spread his hands as if to say, *What'd you expect?* He'd tell him what he expected the very first chance he got.

Callie stood to one side, Bodie next to her. The little one had her thumb in her mouth. She looked all legs suddenly, as if she'd spurted up in a blink. Stark remembered Bel at that stage. She'd seemed to grow an inch in her sleep every night. The thought made him want to smile, but now was not the time.

He walked across the room and reached for Meredith's arm. She pulled away. He felt as if he'd been stabbed in the heart, and he'd done the same to her just yesterday.

"Babe, I'm sorry," he said, and this time when he reached for her, she came, falling into his chest with a soft sob. "Meredith, don't," he pleaded. "It's not your fault. We're going to find them."

She looked up then, her beautiful face absolutely ravaged by tears. Obviously, she'd been crying for hours, and not just because of the missing children.

"Oh, babe," he said, bringing his forehead to hers. "Never again. I promise."

Clasping the tops of his shoulders, she started to cry again. "What if we can't find them?"

"We will," he insisted. "Listen to me. Would Donovan have tried to go home across the fields? There are places on the west end of the ranch where you can see the Pryor house, and Dean has worked those fields. If Donovan was with him—"

"And Donovan was always with him," Callie put in excitedly.

"He might have thought he could get home faster that way than going by the road."

"There are gullies across that range," Meredith said with a gasp. "You can't see them until you practically ride into them, but they're there—deep, backwash gullies—and Little Cow Creek runs through there. It'll be a trickle now, but the ground is so sandy that the banks are ten or twelve feet deep in places."

"I'm going to saddle a horse," Stark said, turning for the door.

"Two," Meredith instructed, running for the stairs. "I'll be right there!"

"I'll put together some supplies," Callie said, heading to the kitchen.

At the same time, Wayne strode after Stark, saying, "I'll help with the horses."

That suited Stark fine. As soon as they reached the trees, Stark demanded, "Just what did you think you were doing back there?"

"You mean was I hitting on your girl?"

Stark stopped and folded his arms. "Were you?"

"She was upset, Stark."

"I know." He grimaced. "I upset her."

"And then didn't stick around to comfort her."

"So you stepped into the job."

"Someone had to."

"If it happens again," Stark began, but then Wayne grinned.

"You'll be there to take care of it. For a while, I was afraid you were going to throw her away."

Stark heaved a sigh and pushed a hand through his hair. "I'm trying to figure out how to do this again, Wayne. It's not been easy."

"I know, but I'm glad you're working on it." Wayne clapped him on the shoulder. "The fact is, big brother, I came to tell you that I'm getting married."

Stark gaped at him. "You're getting married?"

"About time, don't you think?"

"To who?"

"Her name's Phyllis. She teaches at the same school I do. Whole family loves her. Well, everyone but you because you don't know her. Because you can't be bothered with us anymore."

"That's not true."

"That's what it feels like."

Stark sucked in a deep breath and swallowed the lump in his throat. "I'm sorry, Wayne. Losing Cathy and Bel wrecked me." He shook his head and reached deep for honesty. "I *let* losing Cathy and Bel wreck me. It was just easier not to feel and that meant not remembering any more than I had to. And that meant staying away from everyone and everything that reminded me of them. Coward's way out. I'm done with that. I'm done with it."

"Does that mean you'll be my best man?" Wayne asked hopefully.

Stunned, Stark felt tears burning the backs of his eyes. This was life. This was living. Even if the worst happened, life had to go on. Wayne deserved his shot at happiness. Every life contained great grief and great joy, if only we could be brave enough to grasp it all. Stark nodded.

"Yeah. I'm happy for you. And I'm scared for you, to be honest. But I'm also honored to be your best man."

Wayne smiled. "Okay. Welcome back, man. I've missed you." Then he hugged him.

Stark tried not to crack Wayne's ribs when he hugged him back. "Let's go find those kids."

He ran to the stable, picked two geldings and chose tack. Wayne wasn't a rider, but he could follow instructions. All Stark had to do was fit the bits, tighten girths and fasten buckles. He led the horses out into the corral and through the gate. While Wayne held the reins, Stark snagged his hat from the truck. By that time, Meredith had arrived, carrying saddlebags.

He strapped the bulging bags behind her saddle. As he boosted her up into the saddle he said, "You look pretty cute in that hat."

She frowned and muttered, "Tell me that *after* we find the kids."

He was going to tell her a lot more than that and hope—pray—it was enough.

Meri could only hope and pray that Stark was right about Donovan deciding to walk across the pasture to get home rather than take the road. She couldn't let herself think about anything other than that right now. Part of her wanted to rejoice that Stark had apologized and even made a promise of sorts, but her worry and guilt wouldn't let her focus on that.

She had to know that Donovan and Jeanie Ruth were safe. If anything happened to them, she'd never forgive herself. How could she possibly be happy again knowing she had caused either of them harm?

A few hundred yards down the road, they went through the west gate. As a girl, her friends had always talked about how big the

Straight Arrow was, but it had never seemed that big to her. Though she'd spent most of her time at the house in the kitchen with her mom, she'd driven or ridden all over the ranch with her dad, and she and her siblings had played out here, especially on this west end of the property because there were fewer cattle here.

She hoped the kids had jackets, but there was no way to tell. Unlike yesterday, which had been so warm and still, the breeze today had a definite bite to it. Surely they hadn't struck out in their pajamas. They hadn't left them behind, but that didn't mean they were wearing them. Did it? She just didn't know what to think at this point.

Suddenly she saw something moving in the grass, and pointed. "Look."

Stark stood in the stirrups. "Digger!" he called. "Digger! Here, boy!"

Her heart in her throat, Meri threw herself off the horse and tossed her reins to Stark. Hurrying out several yards, she went down on her haunches just as the dog showed, its tongue lolling out of its mouth. It came straight to her and jumped up onto her knee, nearly knocking her over, yipping excitedly. Then Digger turned and raced away. Shooting to her feet, Meredith called it back.

"Digger! Where's Donovan? Where is he?"

The dog showed itself again, barking piercingly. Then it was off again.

"We should follow," Stark said.

She caught her reins, saying, "Go. Go! I'll catch up."

He heeled his bay and went off after the dog, while she pulled and hopped her way up into the saddle.

When she caught up with Stark, he was standing in his stirrups again, scanning the landscape. "I've lost him."

Meri tried calling the dog and Donovan, too, but succeeded only in causing the horses to shy and wheel. They rode on in the general direction of the Pryor place. When they came to Little Cow Creek, they found a spot to dismount and water the horses, tying the reins to an overhanging tree branch, while Stark called the house on his mobile phone. Meri was too sick at heart to do it.

No one had found any sign of the children.

Meredith covered her face with her hands, praying desperately, "Dear God, help us. What do we do?"

"That's a start," Stark said. Going down on one knee there in the dirt, he clutched her hand and pulled her down beside him, wrapping his arm around her shoulders. He bowed his head and said, "Lord, You've tried and tried to show me Your will, and I've kicked and fought and closed my eyes like the fool and the coward I am. And just look where that's gotten us. This is all my fault. Forgive me, and help me put it all right. We need Your help here. Please. For those kids and my folks, for everyone I love, especially Meri."

She gasped. "Stark!"

He made a disgusted sound and got to his feet, hauling her up with him and saying, "I can't even do that right. But you know it's true, babe. You have to. I've never made such an idiot out of myself over a woman before. I love you so much it…"

"Scares you," she supplied, seeing it flicker behind his eyes.

"You have no idea."

She lifted a hand to his prickly cheek. "Given the kind of loss you've suffered," she began.

"I should be able to face anything this world throws at me," he stated flatly, seizing her by the upper arms, "and if I weren't such a coward I'd already have grabbed you."

"Don't say that about yourself."

"It's the truth. I love you, Meri. Do you hear me? I love you more than I thought possible, more than I ever imagined I could love someone. And I used Jeanie Ruth as an excuse to push you away. Because I'm so afraid of losing you."

"You don't *have* to lose me," she said in a quavering voice, "because, you know, I love you, too."

He pulled her into his arms. "I did figure that out. Thank God I'm not totally stupid. It finally hit me that losing you is losing you, no matter how it might happen. My brother said I was throwing you away. He was right. Forgive me."

"Done," she said, smiling. "It's partly my own fault, anyway. I pushed too hard."

"No," he insisted. "You dragged me up out of the grave, Meri. I'd buried myself in grief, and you pulled me back into the land of the living. Don't blame yourself."

"There's just one thing." She pulled back, looking up at him. Best get this out in the open, too, before her nerve failed her. "I can't imagine being married and not having children."

"Not having them is the same as losing them, isn't it?" he said, smiling crookedly. He tapped her on the end of the nose. "Not totally stupid."

She wrapped her arms around him, elated,

despite the worry nagging her. Suddenly he stiffened.

"There," he said, pointing. "The dog. Over there."

Meri ran for the horses, Stark beside her. "Hurry!"

He threw her into the saddle, yanked their reins free, breaking the branch in the process, and mounted up. They raced off in the direction Stark pointed. Soon Meri spotted the dog herself. A few minutes later, they lost the dog again, but they heard what sounded like angry wails coming from a fissure in the ground that Meri knew well.

"Thank You, God!" Meri exclaimed.

Stark took out his phone and called Rex again. "We've found them. Haven't laid eyes on them yet, but we hear them. Call you again in a minute."

Meri felt dizzy with relief. "Please God, let them be okay."

As they rode closer, they heard Donovan speaking. "Will you pipe down? We ain't lost zactly. We're just in a canyern. Now it's light, we'll get up the other side and see how to get home."

"I don't want to get up the other side," Jeanie Ruth declared. "I'm cold! The wind is winter! And there's dirt in my shoes!"

"That's why we wear boots," Donovan pointed out.

"I hate it out here!" Jeanie Ruth cried. "We shouldn't have come out here."

"It was your idea," Donovan reminded her. "You said you knew the way."

"I do. 'Cept Digger wouldn't go by the road, and you was afraid your granny would hear us."

At the sound of his name, the dog disappeared into the sandy crevice in the ground. Stark reined his horse to a standstill and leaned an elbow against the saddle horn, shaking his head and grinning, as the kids continued to bicker. Jeanie Ruth accused Digger of abandoning them, and Donovan hotly defended his pet. They seemed completely unaware of their rescuers. Stark walked to the edge of the crevasse, which appeared stable enough, and hunkered down. Meredith rode a little closer so she could see into the space. It wasn't terribly deep, but in the dark, the children wouldn't have known that. Now, Jeanie Ruth was apparently refusing to budge. It was clear that they had donned their clothing over their pajamas, and they were both dirty and scratched, but if either was injured, Meri couldn't see how.

"Having fun?" Stark finally said, startling

both of them. Jeanie Ruth, who'd had her back to him, jumped a foot high, her eyes wide as saucers.

"Uncle Stark!"

"Out for a little midnight stroll, were you?"

"We fell into a hole," Donovan admitted, sheepishly looking up at Meredith.

"I see that," she replied calmly. "Are you hurt?" He shook his head, looking down again. Meredith threw her leg over the saddle and hopped down off the horse. "Anyone thirsty? Hungry?"

Donovan nodded hopefully.

"Let's get you out of there," Stark said. He sent Meredith a speaking glance. She led the horses away, and he stretched out on his belly, reaching down a hand. After a moment's hesitation, Jeanie Ruth crossed over and put her hand in his. Stark pulled her up and over the edge. She'd torn the knee of her knit pants and chewed up the pajamas beneath, but Meredith didn't think she'd actually hurt herself. Stark pulled up Donovan next.

He had the good sense to appear thoroughly chastened, but Jeanie Ruth tried to brazen it out, lifting her chin and swiping hair out of her face. "I s'pose we're in trouble."

"Oh, yeah," Stark said.

"But that's up to others," Meredith told

them. "Let me get you something to eat and drink, then we'll head back."

Stark stepped away a few feet and pulled out his phone again, while Meredith dug into the saddlebags. As they ate, sitting cross-legged on the ground, Donovan explained that they'd thought it would be "funny" to go to bed in one house and "wake up" in the other.

"Since you wouldn't let him sleep with his dog," Jeanie Ruth accused.

Meredith looked around for the dog, which had disappeared again. "I'm sorry about that, Donovan. Digger is always welcome at the Straight Arrow."

Donovan said glumly, "It's okay. We shouldn't of took off."

"No," Meredith agreed. "You shouldn't have. You could have been seriously hurt. And I can't promise you won't suffer repercussions. But I'm sorry I upset you, and I'm glad you're both okay."

"I'm sorry, too, Aunt Meri," he said in a froggy voice, swiping at his eyes.

"You're going to cry *now*?" Jeanie Ruth demanded.

"You were crying earlier," Stark pointed out, dropping down beside her.

"Was not!" she lied defensively.

"We heard you," he told her, knocking his shoulder against hers. Unprepared for the contact, she rocked sideways, nearly toppling over before she caught herself.

"I—I was just pretending."

"You were scared," he refuted bluntly, "and you should've been. Maybe you still should be. Your Granny Andi is spitting fire." Jeanie Ruth looked shocked. "You've probably never seen her really angry," Stark said, "but I have. You forget that she raised me. And your mama."

That set Jeanie Ruth back a step or two and gave her something to think about on the ride back to the house. Stark put Jeanie Ruth in the saddle in front of him and Donovan on the back behind Meredith.

After he boosted Meri into place and she was gathering her reins, he caught her stirrup and said, "By the way, I was wrong about that hat. Cute doesn't cover it. *Ravishing*. That's the word."

Laughing, Meredith wheeled around her mount and headed home.

"None the worse for wear," Dr. Alice Shorter announced, shepherding the two pint-size miscreants and their female escorts out onto the front porch.

Wes had called the doctor to the ranch just in case the children had suffered some harm from their misadventure. Both wore clean clothes and sported freshly combed hair now. Jeanie Ruth's had been plaited into two tight braids, which Stark knew she hated. Clearly, her grandmother was not yet in a forgiving mood.

Sitting on the porch swing side by side, he and Meri had recounted to the others how they'd found the pair and what had apparently sent them traipsing off across the countryside in the dark of night. Now he naturally rose to offer his seat to his mother. Meri did the same for Dr. Shorter, a well-dressed middle-aged woman with a solid figure and long blond hair worn in a neat twist.

Ann walked Donovan over to his father, who leaned against the porch rail. An unusually docile Jeanie Ruth went to stand with her grandfather and Uncle Wayne, while Callie occupied a spot next to Rex. He leaned a shoulder against the house, Bodie playing quietly at his feet with Wes, who crouched beside her, pushing a toy tractor back and forth.

"Playdate is canceled," Ann decreed.

"And we will talk about other restrictions when we get home," Dean promised.

Donovan merely nodded, shamefaced, but Jeanie Ruth, as expected, squawked.

"That's not fair! I won't never get to see Donovan's tree house."

"You'll have other opportunities to play in Donovan's tree house," Stark told her, resting against the upright porch support. Meredith leaned against him.

"Mama won't never let me come back here!" Jeanie Ruth predicted.

"After you ran away, could you blame her?" her grandmother asked. Jeanie Ruth folded her arms mulishly.

Stark shook his head. "Your mother will bring you back here. You and Donovan will have lots of opportunities to play together after Meri and I are married."

Obviously, he should've thought before dropping that bomb, but in his mind it was settled. The peace of it had permeated all the way to the marrow of his bones. True, he and Meri hadn't related their personal declarations to everyone, but it was right there for everyone to see. Wasn't it?

Apparently not, given the way they'd all stiffened and now stared at them, slack-jawed.

"Guess we left that part out," he muttered, feeling Meri's silent laughter.

Suddenly, his mother burst into tears, while his father and Wes high-fived each other, laughing.

Wayne spread his arms, declaring, "Two Burns weddings in one year!"

"One year!" Stark yelped. "We're not waiting *that* long."

Meri turned her head to look at him. "I'm no spring chicken," he argued. "We've got catching up to do."

She raised her eyebrows and looked at her sister, who raised *her* eyebrows. It didn't matter to Stark—he wasn't waiting that long. He looked at Wayne. "When are you and Phyllis getting married?"

"September."

"September of next year? We are *not* waiting that long."

Someone sniggered. He had the feeling it was Rex, but he didn't care. He meant to have his way in this. Meri pulled away then, turning to face him, her hands at her waist.

"Aren't you forgetting a little something, Dr. Burns?"

Dr. Burns? "You know I didn't mean it when I fired you."

"This is something you *haven't* done."

Something he *hadn't* done?

"In fact, I believe I was the one to mention a certain subject," she hinted.

He frowned, thinking back. When it hit him, he smacked himself in the forehead. Straightening, he walked her back a couple steps. Then he went down on one knee, right there on the edge of the porch.

"Oh, wow," said Ann.

Meredith giggled. "This isn't necessary."

He held up a hand, forestalling further protests. If he was going to do this thing, he should do it right. "No ring, but we can fix that by nightfall." He took her hand in his and looked up at her. "You ready?" She nodded, beaming. His heart felt too big for his chest. "I love you," he said, ridiculously happy. "Gloria Meredith Billings, will you—"

"Yes!" she exclaimed, hopping up and down. They were both laughing because she hadn't even let him finish.

Then she threw herself at him. He caught his elbow on the edge of the porch post, and that was enough to send them both toppling backward onto the ground. Gathering her close, he kept her from harm—as he always would—while she pecked kisses all over his face. The others rushed over to help them up, but it took some time with all the laughing and applauding.

In his head, he was already building her a house and talking to his father-in-law about those horses he needed to buy and planning those babies she wanted. Not one. Not just one this time. A houseful.

What memories they would make, treasures to hoard with those he already had, love to add to what he'd already been given. So much. Such riches.

More than one man could ever deserve.

Enough for a long lifetime of gratitude.

Epilogue

Wes loved a Christmas wedding. It was difficult to believe his girls had pulled off such an elaborate and beautiful ceremony in only a month's time, but then they were an eager bunch. Callie had married his son, Rex, within days of accepting his proposal. Ann hadn't let the preacher pronounce her married before she'd kissed her groom, and that on the very day they'd decided to wed, but then Ann and Dean's wedding had been a surprise cooked up by Rex. Meredith hadn't let Stark even get his proposal out before she'd accepted him, not that the outcome had been in doubt.

Apparently everyone in the family had recognized the attraction well before either Stark or Meri had. What the family hadn't known was why the pair had resisted the initial pull between them. Wes had gone to his room and wept, as he hadn't wept since his wife had died, after Meredith had told them, with Stark at her side, about the brutal attack that had nearly taken her life.

To think that a daughter of his could have suffered and overcome such pain and fear without his aid had humbled and broken him. It had also shown him that his youngest daughter possessed a kind of strength for which he'd never given her credit. She was sweet, kind, smart and caring, yes, but also dogged and unbreakable, the perfect combination of Gloria Jollett and Wesley Billings. Exactly what he should have expected.

Meri looked stunning in her mother's wedding gown. Gloria would be so pleased. Callie had said they'd hardly had to make any alterations. The veil hadn't been usable, but the new one suited Meri beautifully.

Stark couldn't smile wide enough when he saw her. He was the very definition of the eager bridegroom. Meri had laughed happily all the way down to the altar, where her sisters and Stark's awaited her in emerald green velvet. All the men wore Western-styled tuxedoes with white shirts, string ties and black boots, their red rosebud boutonnieres matching the bridal bouquet and the long-stemmed roses carried by the bridal attendants. Simple, elegant.

Instead of flowers, however, the church was decorated with gold-and-silver netting intertwined with twinkling lights and evergreens boughs. Stark had surprised everyone by having the reception catered by a restaurant out of Oklahoma City. They'd set up heated tents on the church grounds and were even now preparing the meal.

Stark had turned out to be exceptionally well fixed financially and had leased a house in War Bonnet while he and Meri built a place of their own. From now on, the clinic would be just that—a clinic.

Having given his daughter's hand in marriage to this good man, Wes walked back to his seat, smiling at Marvin and Andi Burns on the way. Marvin couldn't stop grinning and Andi couldn't stop crying. Well, they had a right to be happy. They all did.

Not so long ago, Wes had been a man alone, sitting on a big piece of property wondering why. Now his prodigal children had all come home to stay and were building families of their own.

He wished their mother could be here to see it, but had she been here when he'd taken ill, none of this would have happened. They'd all have trusted Mom to take care of him, and rightly so.

God had made other plans.

He thanked God for the disease that had brought them all back.

Cancer was a terrible thing, but it had been worth it. Even if the illness had taken his life, it would have been worth it to see his children home and happy.

But it hadn't taken his life. He still had some living to do, and lots of reasons to do it.

He looked at Rex and Callie and thought of the baby that Callie carried. Little Bodie, sitting with her other grandpa now, had made such an adorable flower girl.

He looked at Dean and Ann and thought of the baby that she carried. Donovan made the world's best ring bearer. As he'd told Jeanie Ruth, he'd had experience. She and her cousins had lit candles before the ceremony, and a fine job they'd done of it, even if Jeanie Ruth had insisted on lighting more than her fair share.

He heard a sniff behind him and turned slightly to see Dr. Alice Shorter, in church for the first time in probably years. She looked lovely in a gold satin suit the very color of her hair, her eyes filled with tears as she watched his daughter join her life to that of Stark Burns.

Wes smiled to himself.

Yes, he had many reasons to live and much thanks to give to a loving God Who worked His will in myriad and mysterious ways.

* * * * *

If you loved this story,
check out the other books from
author Arlene James's miniseries
THE PRODIGAL RANCH

THE RANCHER'S HOMECOMING
HER SINGLE DAD HERO

Or pick up these other stories of
small-town life from the author's
previous miniseries
CHATAM HOUSE

THE DOCTOR'S PERFECT MATCH
THE BACHELOR MEETS HIS MATCH
HIS IDEAL MATCH
BUILDING A PERFECT MATCH

Available now from Love Inspired!

Find more great reads at
www.LoveInspired.com

Dear Reader,

Grief is a tough, horrific, unavoidable part of life. Everyone deals with grief in his/her own way. Some ignore it; some wallow in it. Some soldier on, never quite whole or healed. For some, grief becomes a way of life.

When it comes to the death of a loved one, I find it helps to try to look at things from the perspective of the one who has passed on. How would he/she want me to go forward? Would one who loves me want me to forever be sad, guilt-stricken or lonely?

I'm reminded that Christ, though living, sent the Holy Spirit to comfort, strengthen and guide us when He removed His physical presence from this world. Won't He also, then, send us new love when the old must leave us?

I believe so.

But we have to find the courage—like Stark Burns—to accept it.

God bless,
Arlene James

Get 2 Free Books,
Plus 2 Free Gifts—

just for trying the
Reader Service!

YES! Please send me 2 FREE Love Inspired® Suspense novels and my 2 FREE mystery gifts (gifts are worth about $10 retail). After receiving them, if I don't wish to receive any more books, I can return the shipping statement marked "cancel." If I don't cancel, I will receive 4 brand-new novels every month and be billed just $5.24 each for the regular-print edition or $5.74 each for the larger-print edition in the U.S., or $5.74 each for the regular-print edition or $6.24 each for the larger-print edition in Canada. That's a savings of at least 13% off the cover price. It's quite a bargain! Shipping and handling is just 50¢ per book in the U.S. and 75¢ per book in Canada.* I understand that accepting the 2 free books and gifts places me under no obligation to buy anything. I can always return a shipment and cancel at any time. The free books and gifts are mine to keep no matter what I decide.

Please check one: ☐ Love Inspired Suspense Regular-Print ☐ Love Inspired Suspense Larger-Print
(153/353 IDN GLW2)   (107/307 IDN GLW2)

Name   (PLEASE PRINT)

Address   Apt. #

City   State/Prov.   Zip/Postal Code

Signature (if under 18, a parent or guardian must sign)

Mail to the **Reader Service:**
IN U.S.A.: P.O. Box 1341, Buffalo, NY 14240-8531
IN CANADA: P.O. Box 603, Fort Erie, Ontario L2A 5X3

**Want to try two free books from another line?
Call 1-800-873-8635 or visit www.ReaderService.com.**

* Terms and prices subject to change without notice. Prices do not include applicable taxes. Sales tax applicable in N.Y. Canadian residents will be charged applicable taxes. Offer not valid in Quebec. This offer is limited to one order per household. Books received may not be as shown. Not valid for current subscribers to Love Inspired Suspense books. All orders subject to approval. Credit or debit balances in a customer's account(s) may be offset by any other outstanding balance owed by or to the customer. Please allow 4 to 6 weeks for delivery. Offer available while quantities last.

Your Privacy—The Reader Service is committed to protecting your privacy. Our Privacy Policy is available online at www.ReaderService.com or upon request from the Reader Service.

We make a portion of our mailing list available to reputable third parties that offer products we believe may interest you. If you prefer that we not exchange your name with third parties, or if you wish to clarify or modify your communication preferences, please visit us at www.ReaderService.com/consumerschoice or write to us at Reader Service Preference Service, P.O. Box 9062, Buffalo, NY 14240-9062. Include your complete name and address.

LIS17R2

HOMETOWN HEARTS

YES! Please send me **The Hometown Hearts Collection** in Larger Print. This collection begins with 3 FREE books and 2 FREE gifts in the first shipment. Along with my 3 free books, I'll also get the next 4 books from the Hometown Hearts Collection, in LARGER PRINT, which I may either return and owe nothing, or keep for the low price of $4.99 U.S./ $5.89 CDN each plus $2.99 for shipping and handling per shipment*. If I decide to continue, about once a month for 8 months I will get 6 or 7 more books, but will only need to pay for 4. That means 2 or 3 books in every shipment will be FREE! If I decide to keep the entire collection, I'll have paid for only 32 books because 19 books are FREE! I understand that accepting the 3 free books and gifts places me under no obligation to buy anything. I can always return a shipment and cancel at any time. My free books and gifts are mine to keep no matter what I decide.

262 HCN 3432 462 HCN 3432

Name	(PLEASE PRINT)	
Address		Apt. #
City	State/Prov.	Zip/Postal Code

Signature (if under 18, a parent or guardian must sign)

Mail to the **Reader Service:**
IN U.S.A.: P.O. Box 1867, Buffalo, NY. 14240-1867
IN CANADA: P.O. Box 609, Fort Erie, Ontario L2A 5X3

* Terms and prices subject to change without notice. Prices do not include applicable taxes. Sales tax applicable in NY. Canadian residents will be charged applicable taxes. This offer is limited to one order per household. All orders subject to approval. Credit or debit balances in a customer's account(s) may be offset by any other outstanding balance owed by or to the customer. Please allow 4 to 6 weeks for delivery. Offer available while quantities last. Offer not available to Quebec residents.

Your Privacy—The Reader Service is committed to protecting your privacy. Our Privacy Policy is available online at www.ReaderService.com or upon request from the Reader Service.

We make a portion of our mailing list available to reputable third parties that offer products we believe may interest you. If you prefer that we not exchange your name with third parties, or if you wish to clarify or modify your communication preferences, please visit us at www.ReaderService.com/consumerschoice or write to us at Reader Service Preference Service, P.O. Box 9062, Buffalo, NY. 14240-9062. Include your complete name and address.

HHBPA17

READERSERVICE.COM

Manage your account online!
- Review your order history
- Manage your payments
- Update your address

We've designed the Reader Service website just for you.

Enjoy all the features!
- Discover new series available to you, and read excerpts from any series.
- Respond to mailings and special monthly offers.
- Browse the Bonus Bucks catalog and online-only exculsives.
- Share your feedback.

Visit us at:
ReaderService.com

RS16R